Darkness and Dawn

Terry Hooker

Published by Blue Dahlia Publishing House, 2023.

This is a work of fiction. Similarities to real people, places, or events are entirely coincidental.

DARKNESS AND DAWN

First edition. September 1, 2023.

Copyright © 2023 Terry Hooker.

ISBN: 979-8223539384

Written by Terry Hooker.

Also by Terry Hooker

Devil's Land Stories
Ides of May
Dog Days

Tales from Forgotten Gods
Clio & The Missing God

Standalone
Darkness and Dawn

Table of Contents

Dedicated to my three M's

Mike, thank you for always supporting me in all I do.

Mikey, thank you for ignoring me while I yell at my writing.

Mo, thank you for the support and love and for always being a sounding board for ideas.

Love you all.

Special thanks to Julie, Lori, Char, and Mo for all the feedback.

Couldn't have done this without you.

Two you really are the best cat around!

PROLOGUE

From the early 1720's the idea of witches had overtaken Europe. They were hunted down and persecuted throughout the continent. Scotland, Germany, and Hungry were actively hunting witches at the time that the Casket Girls were being sent to the New World from France. Though France had fewer witch trials than most, the Cadiér family from Toulon was persecuted and hunted up until the 1730's.

Catherine Cadiér was a catholic nun who was under the guidance of Jean Baptist-Girard. Catherine made accusation of abuse, to which Girard and his church had her held and tried as a witch in January of 1731.The church found her guilty and recommended death. In a twist that would make this one of the most infamous witch trials in history, she was later released, October of 1731, after being found to be innocent and under duress from her spiritual advisor.

Catherine had turned the tables on the priest who had accused her. She accused him! It was almost unheard of for a woman to accuse a man, let alone a man of the cloth. The trial was one that would have been televised had it happened in this day and age. The Parliament was divided, half of them wanted to hang Cadiér still, while the other half wanted to burn Girard at the stake. They came to a compromise and acquitted both of them.

PART ONE: THE JOURNEY

Chapter One

The carriage ride across the country was not pleasant in the least. Why mother thought it was necessary to get her out of the country, and all of Europe at that, Damica could not fathom. But mother had made arrangements to send her to the new colony of New Orleans. Damica was excited for this new adventure, but the trepidation of not knowing anyone and leaving her mother and aunts behind brought a tremble to her belly.

"Mademoiselle," the carriage man's voice woke her from her reverie, "we have arrived in La Rochelle. Your mother has made arrangements for you to stay at the convent for the night. The ship leaves tomorrow. Is there anything else I can do for you?"

Damica stepped out of the carriage with the hand of the man for balance. At five foot two, she was a little bit of a thing. Most people thought she needed a hand and were only more than happy to lend her one. Her pale skin and hazel eyes made quite a contrast to her dark brown hair with the deep, dark blue highlights weaved through it. The bridge of her nose was covered in a smattering of freckles, and the aura of youth permeated the air around her. At fifteen years old, she wasn't quite a child but still not yet a woman, though, in society, she was of marriageable age.

"No sir, what do I owe you?" she said as she started to rummage through her bag.

"Nothing Mademoiselle Cadiér, your family has done so much for mine already. This trip was payment in kind. Please be safe. I will let your mother know you made it in one piece." He lifted her *cassette* with her belongings from the back of the carriage. He carried it into the convent, nodding to the mother superior as he went.

Damica glanced around the small town, about the same size as Toulon, where her journey had started, but the streets here were all straight and regular. Up on each building, looking down, were gargoyles of differing dreadfulness. Damica could not take her eyes away from them. There were so many.

"Evil," growled a voice.

Damica surveyed around and realized it was the Mother Superior who had spoken.

"Excuse me?" Damica replied. Not quite sure if she was calling Damica evil or something else. It wouldn't be the first time someone had called her evil.

"The gargoyles. Evil things. Set there by ungodly people." The nun said, "I am Mother Superior Catherine. You are welcome here for the night."

The dark clothes of the nun were nothing compared to her dark countenance. Damica was unsure if this was the safest place for her, but her mother had made all the arrangements. She sighed and nodded a thank you.

"Your ship will be delayed; it will not leave until tomorrow evening. Supplies are running late." Mother Superior said curtly. She then turned with a swoosh and entered the abbey. Damica gave one last glance to the gargoyles and stepped inside as well.

The abbey was dark, nothing like the bright, cheery home she had left. There were scarce candles to light the way and no other humans to meet as they moved through the cold stone halls. Nothing moved, not a wisp of air or the scratching of a mouse. The smell of dampness surrounded Damica, though the air did not feel damp. Her hand brushed the wall and came back dry. It was an odd sensation to smell dampness in the air but to not have evidence of it anywhere.

"You will stay in your room until called tomorrow. We will bring you food. There will be no talking, no wandering. Lights go out at eight."

"I have brought a book. If that's alright, that I read a bit?"

"The holy bible is the only book we read here. You can sit and contemplate your journey."

They stopped at a dark heavy wood door with a black metal handle. "Here is where you will stay."

She opened the lock with a large black key. The room was dark, but the nun walked in with no hesitation. She lit one candle, turned, nodded, and left. Damica heard the key lock the door behind her. It took all that was in her to not stick her tongue out at the closing door.

Well, this is pleasant, she thought sarcastically. At *least she didn't take my book.* She settled herself on the small hard bed, bringing the candle closer as she undid her shoes.

"I will sleep clothed tonight, I believe. There is no way I want to be caught unclothed by that woman." She spoke out loud to herself before she opened one of the books her mother had sent with her when there was a light knocking on the door.

Knowing that it had been locked and that whoever was knocking must know that as well and was just being polite, Damica said "Come in," but did not get up from the small bed to let them in.

The door opened to a young nun with a shiny pink face and a great big smile. She carried in a small bowl of what looked to be stew, with a glass of wine and some crusty bread.

"Hello, mademoiselle. I was told to bring you some supper. I hope you're hungry." The smile was contagious, and Damica smiled right back as she swung her legs off the bed and placed her book open, face down, on the floor.

"What is that your reading, mademoiselle?" Asked the young nun.

"A gardening book my mother sent with me; would you like to see it?"

"Oh, could I? I love books, but they are frowned upon here." The smile was gone, replaced by an adorable scowl. Damica guessed the girl to be about her age. She wasn't quite sure how someone who so clearly brought sunshine with her wherever she went could possibly live in such a dark place as the abbey.

As the girl looked at the book, she talked. Nonstop. Which made Damica smile.

"Oh, these pictures are beautiful. Did you draw them? Who wrote this book? Where are you from? Are you really going to Louisiana on the ship tomorrow? Are you going to be a bride when you get there? How long do you think the voyage will last? How did you learn all these remedies? Are they passed on through your family?"

Of all the questions, Damica focused on one. "Bride? Why would I be a bride when I got to Louisiana?"

"Well, that's what this trip is for. Didn't you know that? The Pelican is bringing the third group of girls to the territories to be brides for the settlers there."

Damica just stared at the nun open-mouthed. She did not seem to notice, though, and just continued to prattle on. Damica could not believe that her mother would set her on this path. Not one woman in her family was married. Not one woman depended upon a man to provide for her. They provided for each other, they learned about the land around them, and lived off of it. Yes, there were hardships. Yes, many people called them evil or other nasty things. Okay, maybe her family was known to be healers and help out the townsfolk from time to time with remedies, but Damica had been happy. There was no way she was going to marry, and definitely, no way she would marry a man she had never met!

She sat on her bed for a long time, her supper getting cold. The young nun had eventually prattled herself out and left the room, locking the door behind her. There was no help for it now. She knew she had until tomorrow night to get out of this mess. She might as well get some rest while she could. No telling what tomorrow would bring, hopefully, escape.

Chapter Two

Damica was woken by a pounding on her door. She sat up, confused as to where she was. This was not home. She was still very groggy when the door swung open, and the Mother Superior stepped in, "Get up, girl, the ship is ready to go. You are leaving now."

"But..but, I thought we wouldn't leave until tomorrow night?" The grogginess left Damica confused and shaken. She could not leave now. That left no time to get away from this mess.

"That was the original plan, but the supplies arrived early, and the sea is amicable this night, so the captain is ready to go. Up now."

She stood and watched Damica get herself ready, pack her few belongings and fix up her hair. She then stepped to one side of the door in such a way as to usher Damica out of the room.

She stumbled slightly out the door onto the street. It was dark and wet from the late hour. She glanced up past the lanterns to see the gargoyles. They seemed to sneer at her as she was hustled down to the docks. The night felt heavy, as though something dangerous was in the air.

No time for fancies, thought Damica as she approached the ship, which was enormous! At least thirty-five meters in length, there must have been four levels, including the deck. Damica had never seen anything that large.

She was brought over to stand with a small group of giggling girls, all ready for their adventure. Damica looked around and noticed another small group of girls, none of which were giggling, to the left of the gangplank. This group of girls outright stared at the giggling group.

Damica stared right back, ignoring those around her. The air felt chilled. One girl, in particular, stared directly at Damica, a slight sneer across her lips. The girl ran her tongue between her lips and winked at Damica. She was so taken aback she blinked hard and scowled. The strange girl let out a throaty laugh just as the captain came down to start ushering girls aboard.

"Ladies, welcome aboard the Pelican. This ship has four levels, including the cabins on the deck that will be occupied by myself and my crew. You will have space on the second level. There are two separate areas for you ladies. Please stay within your areas. No changing from one side to the other.

"The deck is a dangerous place to be. No lady should be up on deck unless supervised. If you are up there, there better be a good reason. Now, will the first group of ladies please follow my man here up to where they will be staying. We will set off as soon as everyone is on board."

"Sir," asked one of the girls in the group with Damica, "what is on the other two levels?"

"Supplies, food, other merchandise we are shipping to Louisiana. Nothing to concern yourself with, mademoiselle."

"That seems like an awful lot of supplies," said another girl.

"Yes, mademoiselle, it is," Replied the captain, "We will be at sea for a minimum of two months if the tide and winds are good. Otherwise, six months. The only stop we can make will be an island about a day or so away from our final destination. If we are all to live through this voyage, there must be many supplies. Including fresh water. Water takes up most of one whole level."

Damica and the rest of the girls were ushered onto the ship. As she hurried across the deck, Damica took a long look at the sky, hoping this was not the last time she would see it. Between the idea of being unable to go on deck and the inkling of fear the captain's speech had given her, she thought this might be the last time she gazed upon the stars. She wanted to remember them as they were tonight, the sky clear as could be and the stars themselves bright enough to light the deck without much help from the torches carried by the men bustling around.

"Come along now, mademoiselle. We must be on our way."

"Yes, monsieur." She managed to take one big lungful of the night air before she was ushered into the dark belly of the ship.

The girls with her on the dock were the girls she was to bunk with. They all seemed very young and giggly. Damica wondered what happened to the girls, no, the women since they had all seemed older than her, that had been led in before this group.

She was told to pick a bed, which she did. It was small and neatly made. There was a space for her *cassette* of clothing by the end of the bed. As she sat on the bed, getting her bearings, she felt the ship push off from the moorings. *Well,* she thought, *No turning back now.*

"Oh, I am so excited I can't sleep tonight," said a girl about her age that was in the bed next to her. Damica smiled at her but was not in the mood for mindless chatter.

"Yes, it is exciting. I think I am going to try to get some sleep. Today has been long and exhausting."

The girl seemed disappointed, which made Damica feel guilty for being short with her, "I'm Damica. Maybe we can talk in the morning. It's going to be a long voyage; we should have lots of time to get to know each other."

"Oh yes! I am Marie. Maybe you are right. It may take me a while to fall asleep with the moving of the ship. I think I may try as well."

Both girls settled into their bunks with the chatter of the others around them. Marie hummed a tune quietly while she lay down. Damica thought she might never fall asleep with all the noise, but she dozed off with the sound of Marie's humming in her head.

Damica had strange dreams throughout the night. She dreamt of the other women walking up and down the rows of the sleeping girls. Stroking their hair, whispering quietly in the girl's ears. She saw the same dark woman she had seen on the docks stop at the end of her bunk and smile down at her. Not kindly, more like a predator choosing its prey. When she woke, she was anything but rested. She was the first one awake, she groggily looked around, but nothing seemed out of sorts with anyone. She sighed and flopped back on the bunk.

"Great, I hope this isn't how each night will be. If it is, I may as well turn into a night dweller."

Chapter Three

The days passed slowly. In the first week, they were taught what the routine would be. After they woke for the day, one girl would oversee gathering the food for all the girls on that side. She could bring another girl with her to help her carry the food, but that was it. They were not to go to the other side of the ship, or down to the cargo holds, or on the deck.

Once a day, they would be allowed to come up to the deck, supervised only, to stretch their legs and to get a bit of fresh air. They were not to speak to any one of the crew when they were up there. They were told the voyage was long and they were not to distract the crew. Lunch would be picked up by another girl, as would dinner. They were to stay quiet and calm and never make a fuss. They were to practice their womanly traits, such as sewing and discussing recipes.

They were allowed a small amount of water every three days to bathe with, but they all had to share this water. At no point were they to leave their room at night. This was stressed repeatedly. No night treks to the deck to see the stars or to dream romantically of their future husbands. They were to behave and be quiet. To the crew, they were just another form of cargo, maybe more delicate than most but still cargo.

All Damica could do was groan inwardly at these instructions. For a girl who was used to being outside in the garden or woods, this voyage was going to be torture. She was grateful that her mother and aunts had sent her with a dozen or so books, a smaller *cassette* full of herbs from her garden back home, and a small notebook for her own thoughts. She discovered that most of the girls in the hold could not read or write and that many had been orphaned or abandoned to the church. Some had come from the prisons, but not too many. Rumor had it the last group of girls had all come from the prison, and that had not gone well for the men who were looking for obedient wives.

Damica still could not believe that her mother had sent her on this trek to become some stranger's wife! How could she! Damica was torn between outrage over these actions and sadness at the realization that she would never see her mother again. She tried to remember that her family would only want what was best for her, even if it was a marriage in a far-off country with very little chance of ever seeing them again. She spent nights lying in bed trying to not forget any bit of her mother's face, the smell of her hands after working in the garden, or the sound of her laughter. Many nights she cried herself to sleep, missing her family and her freedom.

Marie hung on Damica and chattered all day. Damica was grateful for the distraction but knew this would get old at some point. She had no time to read or to be with her own thoughts during the days the young girl chattered and giggled and sighed at how romantic the trip was turning out to be. Damica did not think being in a cargo hold for months was in any way romantic. But, she smiled and laughed with the girl, grateful for the optimism.

As the last meal of the day on the fourteenth day or so was brought in, the girls began to settle into their evening routine and start to get ready for bed. Marie even slowed down on the chatter as she would begin to hum herself to sleep. Most of the girls were exhausted from the anticipation of things to come or just from not much movement. It was beginning to catch up to them, and one by one, they fell asleep. Damica sighed at the silence and pulled a lantern closer so she could read just a little bit before bed, trying to find a sense of normalcy in her day. As she read, the words began to drift together, and her eyes got heavy. She was asleep before she could blow out the lantern.

The sounds of whispering woke her, or was she awake? Damica could not tell if she was fully awake or in that land between sleep and waking. She could see, blurrily, all around her, as if her eyes were not fully open, or was she asleep? What she saw did not do anything to let her know one way or another.

In the light of the lantern, she could see the group of women from the dock, the ones that were not bunked on this side of the ship, wandering past the beds of the sleeping girls. On occasion, one would bend down and almost kiss one of the girls.

"Just a sip, just a sip," she could hear whispered through the night.

Damica's bunk was toward the back of the area. The women didn't make it that far before they seemed satisfied with what was done and slowly began to leave. The dark woman walked over to Damica, looked down at her, and smiled. Then blew out the lantern and was gone.

Chapter Four

The trek went on similarly for the next few weeks. Nothing of note took place. The girls woke, got their food, sat and talked, slept, or played quadrille for hours. They all looked forward to their daily walk on deck, some to stare out at the sea dreamily while others to stare at crew members dreamily. Damica was more than likely to be caught standing at the bow of the ship, breathing in the fresh salt air, lost in her own thoughts. Neither the sea nor the crew made her dreamy in any way. She was ready to dig her hands into the soil again, and smelly, dirty men were not of any interest to her.

Three months into the journey, the first death happened.

Damica paid little attention to the other girls besides Marie, who could generally be found in Damicas vicinity, so the first girl to pass was not someone she had known. The girl was older than her, with dark hair and fair skin, though, to be honest, most of the girls were getting fairer and fairer of skin as the journey went on. It took Damica a good ten minutes to come up with the girl's name even, Evangelíne.

There was a small ceremony on deck. The girls and the crew were there. The captain said a few prayers as the dead girl was dumped into the sea. The captain called it being released into the sea, but Damica saw nothing but the dumping of a body so as not to smell up the rest of the ship. Nothing romantic or poetic about it.

As she took one last look around, she noticed that none of the girls from the other side of the ship had made it to the ceremony. She wanted to ask the captain about that or if they were all well, but the captain turned on his heel as the ceremony ended and strode away toward the wheelhouse.

"Did you notice that none of the girls from the other side were there?" Damica mentioned to Marie as they slowly moved toward the stairs back down to their room.

"Oh, I hadn't noticed. How odd. Maybe they just were not interested, or maybe the captain doesn't want them to know what happened if they don't need to." Marie let out a sigh, "I am so broken up over Evangeline. She was a sweet girl. Soft-spoken, not as smart as you, but she could read. She had the most wonderful book of poetry she would read to some of us at times. I am going to miss her." A tear made its way down Marie's face. Though not one for casual touch, Damica put her arm around the girl to comfort her.

"What do you think happened to her?" Asked Damica, "Had she been ill?"

"No, not really. She was getting really pale the last few days. And dizzy she seemed to be dizzy a lot. The last week or so, all she really did was eat and sleep. Though she didn't eat too much, she would often give her meal to one or more of the other girls that were still hungry. She did say something about not sleeping well at night, but, honestly, I just thought that was because all she seemed to do was sleep all day anymore."

The day passed slower than most. Many of the girls sat quietly weeping to themselves. There were no games played or poetry recited. Some spoke in whispered tones to each other. The atmosphere was dreary and sad. As evening approached, the last meal of the day was brought in. Not many of the girls felt like eating it, so much of the food was left untouched. Unlike most nights, many of the girls stayed awake well into the night when exhaustion finally overtook them.

Damica was not tired and sat with the lantern to read and write down some of her thoughts for the day. Her reverie was broken by the sounds of whispers outside the door. She could barely make out the words. She couldn't tell if they were male or female, just that there were people there.

She got out of her bed and quietly strode to the door. Before she could reach it, she heard someone growl. "Shhhh, someone's up!" another voice replied, "How could that be? I made sure to put valerian in all the evening food," silence for a moment, then the growly voice again, "Maybe it didn't work! Maybe you failed!"

Damica hustled back to her bed, knowing now that the speakers were women. She now might understand why so many of the girls slept so well throughout the nights. The food was being drugged. Valerian was a potent herb used to help people that could not sleep or to help put people to sleep who needed to rest for recovery. She knew all this because it was one of the herbs her mother grew in her garden. One that she gave to many people who had issues with sleep or stress.

A lot of thoughts were flying through her head; is this why she always had such strange dreams on the ship, that is, when she did dream. Now that she thought about it, there were few dreams she could remember, which was not normal for her. Damica was a vivid dreamer, all in color, and usually, she could remember it clearly the next day. Many times, she would entertain her mother and aunts with descriptions of her dreams. Damica did not know how to feel at this moment, but she did know that she needed to find a way to stay awake at night from now on. Maybe more naps in the daytime or a bigger lunch so she could skip the evening meal. However she could manage it, she had to figure out what exactly was going on.

Chapter Five

The time passed slowly as the ship sailed toward its destination. No one was quite sure how much time had gone by. Each day was the same.

The morning it was Damicas turn to get breakfast, she headed up to the deck, but as she emerged, there was no room to move. Men were hurrying everywhere. It seemed as though everyone that worked on the ship was on the deck at the same time.

Damica tried to skirt through the crowd. As she shimmied past them, she saw what all the fuss was about. One of the men was lying on the deck, pale as a ghost, his neck all bloody, his eyes wide open staring at the sky. The men scurrying around her were all whispering and muttering to each other, "I told him this was not the cargo we needed to move." "*De put aire*! We never should have agreed!"

Damica moved closer to the man to see if she could help, but the moment she saw the hazy white eyes, she knew he was past anything she could do. The captain spotted her and immediately called for a man to escort her back downstairs, "Wait," she said, "I've come to gather the girls' breakfast. I can't go back empty-handed." The captain relented but told the man to escort her there and back so she wouldn't get lost again.

As they walked, Damica tried to strike up a conversation, "Did you know the man?" she was met with silence. She tried a different tactic, "Was it a shipping accident?"

The man sneered at her, "Not in the typical sense." But that was it. As much as she tried to get him to speak, silence was all she got.

"Well, thank you for accompanying me. I hope all stay safe and well," she took the tray from him and walked into the room with the food.

Her face must have shown that something was wrong because Marie ran right up to her.

"Damica, are you alright? What happened? Why are you so pale? Here sit, sit." She pulled Damica to the bed closest and pushed her gently yet firmly down as she took the tray of food out of her hands.

"One of the men was lying on the deck. He was covered in blood. I'm fairly sure he was dead." The shock of it finally hit her, and she closed her eyes and let out a big sigh. Her shoulders sagged a bit as she tried to keep calm.

She hadn't even known the man. Why was it hitting her this hard? Maybe she was just overly emotional from the death earlier in the journey. Then seeing the dead man today, she tried to quiet her brain and focus on the girls around her. Each one looked frightened. Some were weeping quietly. She knew she had to do something to calm them.

"Maybe it was just an accident. They do happen on a ship this big. I think we all need to eat a bit and maybe rest or play some quadrille. I don't know anything about the game, so maybe some of you could teach me." She forced a smile and took a bite of food. Others followed her example, and soon the girls were all doing their normal daily activities. The only difference to this day was there would be no excursions onto the deck.

Damica was charged with getting all the meals for the day. By the time of the midday meal, the deck and workings of the ship were back to normal. The girls ate this meal with gusto and continued to laugh and play. As evening rolled around, Damica headed back up to gather dinner for them all. She noticed that their food differed from the food set out for the crew. She wondered about this as she carried it back. The hushed conversation she had overheard in the night outside their door was running through her brain.

She decided right there that she would not eat the food sent that night. In fact, she would make sure to have a good strong cup of tea to help her stay awake. Her mother had sent a small medicine bag with some common herbs within, but nothing helped keep sleep away as well as the good old-fashioned caffeine found within the black tea her mother had traded for.

As all the girls finished their meals, Marie looked at Damica quizzically, "Aren't you hungry?"

"Not really. I think I will just have a bit of tea and read. How are you feeling?" She had noticed her friend was pale today and less talkative than usual.

"I'm okay, just tired. I think I will skip the nightly games and lie down. I will see you tomorrow Damica, have sweet dreams." Marie got ready for bed and was asleep before she even hit the pillow. Damica noticed that the girl had eaten every last bit on her plate. Then she looked up and noticed all the girls were settling in early. Almost half were already asleep.

Damica stayed up as late as she could, drinking her tea to keep her awake longer than usual. Unfortunately, the warm invitation to sleep was more powerful than any caffeine, and she succumbed. She fell asleep sitting up with her lantern on. She had not planned to fall asleep, so when the noise of the door opening woke her, she was already in the position to see everything that was happening.

She opened her eyes just enough to see the women from the other side of the ship slip into the room. There were ten of them. Each moved over to a girl who was lying in bed, "Quick tonight, ladies, be quick. Last night was a disaster! The captain is not pleased with us. No more accidents!"

Damica watched them lean over each girl's neck. There had been fourteen girls now down to thirteen, no one approached her. This time someone came right over to Marie, though. Marie's sweet face was smiling in her sleep as the woman leaned over her. Damica could see her gently lick Marie's neck, then like a viper strike.

Damica could not help herself. She shot out of bed yelling, "Get away from her! You demon!" With her book still in her hand from earlier, she struck at the woman who was gnawing on Marie's neck in the side of the head. The book made a thwump sound as it hit, throwing the woman back off the girl. The woman stumbled into the wall of the ship and hissed at Damica. She rushed over to Marie. Her neck was bleeding profusely, and the amount of blood draining onto the cot was shocking. Damica grabbed the girl's bedding and applied pressure to the girl's neck. She looked up to see the other women leering at her as they strolled out of the room. The dark woman from the docks stared at her malevolently, let out a sharp breath, and swooshed out of the room.

Damica held Marie in her arms. Nothing she was doing would stop the bleeding. Their clothing was all soaked through with blood. The other girls were slowly stirring awake. Thank *God,* thought Damica. *Now I can look through my medical bag and see what I have to stop the bleeding.*

The first scream startled Damica so much that she almost dropped Marie's head. She glanced up to see the horror on the other girls' faces, "Please help me. Can someone hold her so I can look for medicine?" No one answered or moved.

Then one of the younger girls took off out the door. Damica sighed, "Please, can someone at least grab my bag over there? She really needs help. I should have something to stop the bleeding, but I'm afraid to let go of the puncture. I don't want it to bleed any more than it already is."

A girl by the name of Cassandra shyly stepped over and asked, "Is this the bag you need?"

"Yes, thank you. Do you mind staying close? I think I may need some hot water and maybe a little lard to mix the herbs with. I could really use the help."

Cassandra nodded, though her lips were in a tight line, and she would not meet Damicas eyes. The other girls had started settling down, except three who were standing as far away from the goings-on as they could get, holding out their crosses toward Damica and muttering prayers.

"If they didn't stop what happened last night, I doubt they will do anything to me," said Damica in an annoyed way, "Though Marie could use all the help she can get, maybe you should say a few prayers for her."

Damica took out her herbs. Her mother had taught her how to organize them so she could quickly grab what she needed without so much as a glance in the bag. She located the yarrow root and sprinkled it on her friend's bleeding neck. It slowed the flow of blood but did not seem to stop it entirely.

"Cassandra, would you happen to have a clean cloth we could use to wash up the wound with?"

Cassandra stepped confidently back toward her area and pulled a clean underskirt out of her *cassette*. "I really do not like this one. You are more than welcome to use it however you need. I can cut it into strips if you'd like."

"Yes, please, that would be wonderful." Damica let out a breath she didn't know she was holding. Having someone help her was a huge relief. She turned her attention back to Marie and noticed the girl was staring up at her. She looked tired and pale, but her eyes were alert as she watched Damica, "Hello friend, it seems there was a small accident. I'm here with you, though. I know a bit about medicine. Can you sit for a bit?"

The girl nodded and tried to sit in her bed. Damica placed a few blankets behind her back and helped her up. "Water." Cassandra headed over with a cup of water and helped Damica give Marie a drink. Marie closed her eyes as she drank and sighed when she was done.

"I do believe that was the best-tasting thing I have ever put to my lips." Then she smiled up at the two girls who were nursing her. The underskirt was sliced up, so Damica dipped a piece in another cup of water and started to wash out the wound better just as the door to the room slammed open. The girl that had run out was there, slightly out of breath still. It seemed like years since she left. She had brought the captain back with her.

He stepped just inside the door and looked from side to side, sliding only his eyes as he glanced. He noticed Marie. How could he not? There was a significant amount of blood now pooled around the young lady, and a few rags soaked through were on the floor by her as well. Damica herself was covered in quite a lot of blood from trying to ebb the flow from the girl's neck. The color drained out of the captain's face, his mouth dropped open a small bit, and his eyes became bulbous as he took in the scene.

"Dammit," he could be heard saying under his breath as he finally started to move toward the girl. "Is she alright? How did this happen?"

Damica sat calmly as the other girls started to jabber about what they had seen. She continued cleaning the dried blood from around the wound. The yarrow root was still mostly doing its job; the bleeding had slowed to less than a trickle.

"So, none of you saw what actually occurred?" She heard the captain say, almost with a sigh of relief.

Still, Damica said nothing. She slid her eyes up at the captain, who was seemed much more confident and self-assured that he had hidden the secret. But Damica knew. She felt as though she had to see how much Marie knew but now was not the time. Damica kept her mouth shut up until the point the oldest of the girls pointed at her.

"She did it! By God is my witness. She is the monster that cut poor Marie!" Still, Damica did not respond. She was used to accusations, after all. She was still looking at the captain, who could not seem to make eye contact with her anymore.

"No, Agnes, it was not I who harmed her, and I do believe that the captain is very aware of that, as well as being aware of what actually happened." Her stare grew colder as she looked at him. The captain began to squirm under such scrutiny she could see the sweat rolling off his forehead.

"Yes, well, all seems good now. The girl seems to be healing up nicely. Let us try to get some sleep, and I will check with you again in the morning."

He turned and took his leave as quickly and gracelessly as possible. The girls were left stunned. They all seemed to turn to Damica as one, some looking at her for leadership and others as though she were the devil himself. All of them seemed confused and scared. It seemed as though only Damica had experience or knowledge about what they were stuck on the ship with.

Chapter Six

Damica did not go back to sleep. She sat with Marie while she figured out approximately how much longer the trip should take. They had been at sea for four months at least, though she wasn't really sure.

Had they been out for five months already? The time seemed different, stuck inside like they were. She tried to count the days but could not. She knew there was at least one more month to go if the tides and winds were good, but it could be as long as three more months.

She was also aware that they would stop at the island of Hispaniola and the French-controlled Saint-Domingue before they arrived at the port of New Orleans. That would happen in, hopefully, a few weeks. She sighed. Weeks of hiding from the monsters on the ship, weeks of trying not to die or see anyone else die.

Damica was not sure what she had in her bag that could protect them all or if she wanted to protect them all. Maybe just herself and Marie were all that she could or would protect.

Marie. She needed to make the bleeding stop completely, or there would be no need to protect the girl. She would eventually bleed out and die. Damica made it her mission to not let that happen, she had few friends in this world as it was, and she was not going to lose the only one that she had made crossing to the new world. She may just need a friendly face once they made it to New Orleans, and they would make it.

The dawn came, not that she could see it, but as she relaxed, she could feel the change in the air. It seemed to sigh with relief. She could hear the men above her begin to move around more. She stretched and looked over at her friend. Marie slept fitfully; the yarrow root seemed to work less and less as the night went on, letting the blood seep then flow lightly from her neck. Damica had some dried rose that she could try next, but she knew she would need to check all her books to see if there was an answer to why the wound kept seeping.

She had not taken out the book that listed the predators to her kind in it. Usually, they were left alone by everyone except the church. Most of the extraordinaire, as her family called those that weren't quite human, kept to themselves, occasionally crossing paths, rarely engaging in any form.

Occasionally a few would fight for territory, but for the most part, the church had put the, no pun intended, fear of god into them. They hid. They tried to blend. They did not draw attention to themselves. The recent events in Scotland and Hungary had led Damicas mother to make the decision to send Damica away. She was concerned the hunts would bleed over into France and that the local church would use this to find and weed out the Cadiére family. It was past time for Damica to find out about the other extraordinaires.

She dug deep down into her *cassette* and pulled out a very large, very old book. She had been surprised when her mother had packed it. It had been in the family for generations, always added on as each woman learned something new. It was an ongoing record of what was out there, with all the up-to-date information they could get.

Her mother had wanted to make sure that it was passed down to her, as well as to let her have a slight advantage, if possible, about what was out in the world. And she wanted Damica to add to it as she learned about new and different extraordinaires in the new world.

There was very little information from France about vampires or revenants, as they were often referred to. Only that of Gilles de Rais in the 1400s. He had been a war hero but a sadist, taking pleasure in torturing young boys. He had been convicted of his crimes, which led to his punishment of beheading before the burning of his body. The problem on the ship did not seem to fit into this category, or at least not that Damica could see.

Thank goodness her relatives had not relied solely on the legends of France; they had often traded information with travelers. France had their own forms of extraordinaires, so it was never difficult to find some tidbit of information that a traveler did not know of or did not know existed in France.

There was an awful lot of information from other parts of Europe. London scientists had done research into grave eating, an act where the revenant would wake in his or her own coffin and begin to eat its shroud as well as its own limbs. *Nope, not what's going on here,* thought Damica, though she might want to research more of this. None of the notes said whether or not the bodies remained in the grave or got up and attacked those that had opened the grave. She made a note to come back to this.

There were notes about travelers from all over Eastern Europe who all reported sightings of vampires or their ilk. There were stories of whole villages being killed by them or of wild vampires stalking travelers on lone roads. The stories would have to wait. Not one of them described what was happening on the ship. Not one of them described female vampires. And not one of them told Damica how to counteract the vampire, especially in such close quarters.

She would have to dig deeper. She flipped to the rear of the book, an area that she had never looked through but one that she had seen her mother refer to a time or two. The newest entry listed garlic as a way to keep vampires away from you, though there was a side note that said it could just be anything with a super strong smell. Damica peeked through her bag of herbs but didn't see anything that would produce a strong smell. She let out an aggravated sigh and continued with her research.

Daylight, well, that could explain why they left at night and why the other girls were not at the funeral for the crew member or the other girl that had passed. Damica made a note that they would be safe as long as the sun was shining.

Mirrors were listed, as well as holy objects. There was a note next to the holy objects listing. It stated that any holy object would do the trick, but only if the person holding or wearing it was a true believer. Damica knew most of the girls wore crosses around their necks. She was curious as to how many and which of the girls had been victims of the vampires already. She was pretty sure she had not been. She wore a small silver tree charm around her neck, one that represented nature and all the elements. She truly believed in its power to protect and guide her, which she was sure was one of the reasons none of the vampires had chosen her.

They would have to find out who truly believed and who did not. As for mirrors, there were a few girls with small handheld mirrors, but for the most part, they were not something that many had access to or something that traveled well.

Damica looked up from her research. The girls were all settling down with a meal. Dinner, she realized. She had lost the whole day in her books! She quickly turned to where Marie was. The girl was resting comfortably, Cassandra by her side.

She glanced up from where she had been checking Marie's bandage and smiled, "You looked so caught up in your books, your face was so serious, that I thought I should just leave you be and tend to Marie myself." Damica smiled and nodded before the girl continued, "It hasn't completely stopped bleeding. She ate a little bit of lunch but then fell into a fitful sleep."

Damica got up and checked the girl's forehead for a fever. If anything, she seemed chilled. She then checked the bandage. Cassandra had changed the bandage and cleaned up the wound again. Damica peeled back the fresh bandage and sprinkled a little Yarrow root mixed with dried rose petal, hoping combining the two would make the wound clot that last little bit it needed.

"Thank you, Cassandra. You don't know how much it means to me to have Marie taken care of with such love. I lost myself a bit today. I will try not to let that happen again. I am famished, though! I cannot wait to eat dinner. Will you come sit with me, and we can eat together."

Damica surprised herself with the invite, she wasn't one to want company often, but after the night before and the contents of the book, she wanted to be near another living being. The girls ate in companionable silence, both keeping an eye on Marie.

As the meal ended, Cassandra asked if she had found anything of interest, her eyes were eager and curious. "I knew you were, at the very least, a healer by the way you presented yourself. Only those with such skills have the confidence that you possess. I am not sure if you are more, but I am hoping you might be. I do believe we are a bit over our heads on the voyage. I do believe some important details were left out when we signed up."

Damica had to repress a chuckle, this was not a laughing matter, but the way the girl had worded the problem had just hit her as amusing. And honestly, Damica could not argue with the girl. There were definitely some things left out when they signed up for the voyage.

Chapter Seven

Damica had intended to stay up and study some more. She had a feeling that what she was looking for was just a page turn away. Something that would protect the room that they were all stuck in. After very little sleep the night before and a full day of reading and studying, followed by the relief that Marie had made it through the day as well as a good hearty meal, it was not long before her eyes were shut, and she was snoring softly.

She wasn't quite sure what woke her. It took her a minute to focus on what she was seeing. She could see someone carrying Marie; she jumped out of bed and yelled: "STOP." The woman carrying her friend turned, her face was contorted like that of an angry cat. She actually hissed at Damica.

Through all her reading today, the only thing she could think to do quickly was to take her tree pendant out of the blouse and hope for the best. The light that emanated from it was blinding. The woman carrying Marie screamed and dropped her, then backed into the corner. By this time, many of the other girls were awake.

"Take out your crosses!" Damica yelled. "Take them out and hold them up."

Many of the girls were sobbing. Most of them took out their crosses and held them up. Damica was not surprised when not all of them began to glow. She took note of the girls that were non-believers; they would have been the ones targeted by the vampires already. She knew she would have to come up with a plan to protect all the girls. She glanced over and was taken aback when she noticed Cassandra's cross not glowing.

"Keep those crosses out, ladies. Let's drive these devils from our space!" The girls advanced on the vampires and drove them out of the door, then they all rushed to Marie, who was unconscious. They gently carried her to bed.

Damica looked closely at Marie's wound on her neck, which had begun to bleed heavily again. She quickly grabbed her bag and tried her mix of yarrow root and rose, but it did little to stop the bleeding. She wrapped it up as gently as she could while the girl moaned in her sleep. Marie's face was sweaty, yet she was cold to the touch. Most of the girls sat on their beds, crying again. Some had a determined look to them, while others just seemed lost and scared.

Cassandra helped Damica cool Marie's fever as best she could. "Damica, I think you better keep reading that book of yours. I pray that there is a solution for us in there. We have a number of weeks left in our journey; I do not wish to die at sea."

Damica took Cassandra's words to heart. She ushered the other girls to put as much furniture as they could spare up against the door. She knew this would not hold off a full-on assault, but she was hoping that it would give a little peace of mind as she did not think they would attack again tonight.

As that thought floated through her mind, she heard the faint screaming from above her. One of the crew must have been attacked. All the girls seemed to hear it, they all looked up toward the ceiling, but no one moved to go see or help. Marie settled down as a smile crossed her lips.

Damica pulled her bag of herbs close to herself and continued to read. This way, she could grab it immediately and not get caught up in the research as she had the day before. *Okay, so rose again, I have that; oh, and wild rose works best...good.*

She smiled until she realized she was a little low on rose. *Blackthorn and Buckthorn and Hawthorne, I have some of those. I wonder if anyone has a cross made of Rowan.*

She took stock of what she had, it wasn't much, but with only one way into the room, she was hopeful that between what she had and the girls' own holy items, they would make it safely to their final destination. She knew that even though the ship would stop before they landed in New Orleans, they had to complete the journey. Some were obligated to pay the debt, and others just needed to get somewhere with a fresh start.

She heard a slight growl and looked over at Marie. The girl's face was contorted into a snarl, then went slack like she was dead. Damica rushed over to her friend. She could see the girl's chest moving slightly as she breathed. Damica let out a sigh of relief.

Just then, there was a loud rapping on the door; all the girls grew frantic and tried to hurry away from the door, looking frightened. Damica stepped toward the door but said nothing.

"It's the captain. The sun has come up. We have another dead crewman. Please, if some of you could come up and help me prepare the body for burial, I would appreciate that."

Damica opened the door, the man that stood in front of her was not the arrogant man that had swept through their room the day before. He looked tired and drawn. It must have been a hard night.

"Yes sir, we will send someone up in a moment once we gather our own wits about us. Should we send someone for food?"

The captain nodded slightly, then turned away. He walked like he had aged at least a decade since yesterday. The girls were already putting the room back in order. Their tizzy from earlier had turned into excitement of having made it through the night. Three of them volunteered to go up and prepare the body, while a fourth and fifth went to gather the food for the morning.

The sailor was put to sea with no pomp and circumstance. The girls came back and reported to the group that his neck had been torn out and that the other sailors seemed to be scared, and morale was bad among the men. On the good side, they had gotten some good winds or currents or whatever was needed to move the ship to its destination quicker. Maybe a week and a half could be taken off their time to Hispaniola if this kept up.

Still a long way off, thought Damica. She decided to speak with the group about their options. They had already been told about the herbs that could be sprinkled around the door frame as well as some that could hang up around the room. She asked if anyone had any mirrors or larger crosses with them. There were three handheld mirrors and one larger cross that had still fit in the girl's *cassette*. It was enough to come up with a plan.

The first part of the plan was to try to get some sleep during the day. They were all exhausted and stressed. Some girls fell right to sleep, some sat up talking quietly. Damica took stock of her herbs one more time before laying down to rest. Cassandra had gone to her bed and was fast asleep, Marie was still in a deep sleep as well.

Damica was concerned Marie had fallen into a coma and would not wake. She lay down on her own bed next to Marie's and was fast asleep within seconds. As the evening drew near, Damica was awakened by Marie whimpering in her sleep. It took her a moment to remember where she was and what was happening. She realized that the day was almost gone, it was time to set up the measures to keep them all safe.

She had the girl whose turn it was to gather the meal go a touch early so they could be done and inside before full dark. They sprinkled the buckthorn around the door frame as best they could, it would have been better to have some to hang on the frame, but all she had in her bag was crushed. They piled most of the beds up against the door, then set the mirrors in such a way as to reflect directly on anyone coming through the door. Then all the girls sat on the mattresses on the floor and waited. Marie's bed was the only one left alone.

Damica must have dozed off a bit. She was startled by the rattling of the door, then a muffled cuss. *Not very ladylike,* thought Damica as she smirked to herself, knowing she had said a lot worse in her life.

There was then a soft knock, and a quiet, soft voice said, "Hello, I need help. Please let me back in." The girls all looked around confused, had they left one of their number outside the door? "Please, I'm scared." The girl on the other side of the door pleaded.

None of the girls in the room moved. They all looked at Damica for guidance. She didn't know each girl individually, but she was almost positive that they were all safe and sound inside. There was a gnawing inside of her that she missed someone. The doubt was washing over her. She was moving aside bed frames when she came back to herself and stepped back.

"No!" she said. Not only out loud but deep within her soul, the way her mother had taught her. She stood still and took a deep breath, feeling the movement of the ship, smelling the unwashed girls in the room with her own scent mixed in, all with an undertone of a coppery smell she could not identify. She took just a moment to find herself again. She could feel the will of someone else pushing against her own.

How she had fallen victim so easily, she could not say. Her mother had made sure she knew how to fight such things off. She turned to see the other girls huddled together, some weeping. Damica let out a sigh. So many weeping girls. She shook her head and turned back toward the door.

"You almost had me," she said out loud, "but not tonight. It will take more than that to get through the door." She stood defiantly staring at the door. The voice on the other side took its sweet time answering her.

"A challenge then. We will wait and see what tomorrow brings." The voice on the other side let out a high-pitched giggle that sent shivers down Damicas back.

Marie mumbled in her sleep. She seemed to hiss out words that could not be deciphered. The air seemed to lighten, and the assembled girls knew they would make it safely through the night. Then an agonizing scream rent the air from above them, another crew member going to his grave.

Chapter Eight

The next day passed quietly. The girls helped to take care of the body, again, and the meals were served as usual. Most of the girls slept throughout the day. Each night from here on out was going to be a trial. Trying to stay alive while hoping and praying that the men above were taking precautions themselves. Damica tried to speak with the captain about what could be done to protect them, but he dismissed her. What could she possibly know? She was a mere girl.

The girls in the hold knew better, though; they knew that their only hope was Damica. They all had much respect for her and her little bag of herbs. As the last meal of the day was brought in, the girls built their fortress of beds to go against the door that Damica had spread fresh buckthorn around. She so wished she had some juniper to hang in the room. That seemed to be one of the best defenses. She would have to see what she could get when they stopped in Hispaniola. Maybe the locals there would have something else they used. She was musing on this thought when she felt a drop in her stomach. The sun had gone down, the night had begun.

The knocking and calling did not start as early as it had the night before. The girls had almost relaxed. There was no screaming from above them. Damica thought perhaps the crew had taken precautions and were staying safe. There was an air of relief among the girls until the knock came.

Three sharp raps on the door. Then a voice, speaking in normal tones, "Hello ladies, let us in. We can talk. Just let us in, wipe away these herbs, invite us in."

The talking went on in this same way for quite a while. At first, the girls were afraid, but soon they began to relax again as they realized they were safe. This was the worst that could be done. The knocking and calling went on for most of the night, but they made it through without incident.

As the sun came up on another day, the girls felt as though they might be able to make it to their destination after all. The herbs and blocked door seemed to be the answer. They settled in for a day of rest with joy in their hearts, happy for some good news.

The evening settled in quietly as the girls started waking and getting ready for the night. They were all in good spirits, sure that their precautions would keep them safe. Hoping the crew was taking some precautions.

It didn't even bother them that they were not getting to go up on deck at all right now. No excursions at night, and they were much too tired to even ask about getting out during the day. They gathered the food for the night and settled in to play games and read. Damica decided to take some more notes out of her books, she wasn't sure how long the herbs at the door would last, but she didn't want to refresh too early since her supplies were limited. The first knock came about ten o'clock.

"Let me in, please." begged the voice on the other side. "I won't hurt you; I would like to visit and play games with you. Please, it is so lonely out here."

The girls ignored the voice. It was fairly easy to do since they were all pretty well wrapped up in their own games for the night, and the furniture piled up at the door muffled a lot of the voice. No one looked up, and no one paid any attention as the voice changed. The tone changed from pleading to determined.

"Come, come little one. I feel you awaken, come to me." The words were spoken as if to a child, Damica looked at the door quizzically. Then the screaming started.

She whirled around to see Marie attacking one of the girls. Cassandra was trying to pull her off the girl. But it was too late. The girl dropped from Marie's grip, her body crashing to the floor. Marie turned to Cassandra and hissed, her gaping mouth full of blood, her eyes solid black. Cassandra backed up against the wall, she took her cross out but

Damica knew it was no use. It had never glowed before; it would not start now.

Damica ran across the room, grabbing the wooden cross as she went and jumped between the girls. Her own charm and the cross held Marie at a distance. She slowly approached her, keeping Cassandra behind her.

"Ladies move slowly behind me; we don't want her turning on any of you." Each girl moved slowly behind Damica, each holding their own cross, with most of them glowing. Just Cassandra's and one other did not. Damica was too distracted to take note of who else was a non-believer. She thought there had been at least four or five last time, of course, being stuck on a ship with vampires may just make a believer out of some of them. They moved slowly toward the door as a collective until they were close enough for Damica to hear laughter from outside.

"What's wrong, dears? Did you perhaps trap a tiger in there with you?" The laughter gradually grew harder and louder. It was eerie to hear the volume build as the laughter became more maniacal. The boards of the ship itself seemed to shake with it.

Damica had moved the ensemble toward her bag of herbs, she reached in and took out some dried rose. The last of what she had, she realized. She had to devise a plan to keep this from turning into a blood bath. Marie was crazy with blood lust. Damica could see it in her eyes. There was no part of this walking corpse that was her friend. The sweet, talkative young girl was replaced with this snarling animal.

"Would you like some help?" Came the sing-song voice on the other side of the door. "I can help you if you just let me in."

Even if she wanted to, that was not an option at this point. The only option was to contain Marie for the night. Then solve the problem in the morning.

"I think we are good," said Damica, "we can contain her ourselves. We will take care of this when the sun is out."

The shriek from the other side of the door made Damica fall back, "Noooo, you will not harm her!" The other girls tried their best to hold on to their crosses and keep Marie at bay, but they were all fighting the effects of the scream.

"What would you propose then? Can we make a deal? We can drag her out into the sun first thing, or we can come up with a compromise."

Damica was getting angry, angry at losing her friend, angry at being stuck on this ship with these monsters, angry at having to go to a new land to be safe. She let out a chuckle and smirked. Yup, this was so much safer than home. So glad she left everything and everyone she loved for this.

"You want to make a deal with me, child? I am older than light itself! Who are you to believe you can even comprehend what I would deal for!" The voice reverberated through the room, the other girls fell back, leaving Damica and Marie the only two standing. Marie cowered and covered her ears.

Damica sighed before she answered. "I am the one that was able to stop you from entering this place. I am the one who holds the fate of this newborn in my hands. Make a deal with me, or don't. It's your call. I have enough herbs to keep us safe until we land."

"Do I bore you?" came the reply.

"A little, yes," Damica answered, though once she said it, she thought that was probably not the smartest thing she could have done, but she was tired of it all. "It's quite simple, I'll give you Marie, and you leave us alone."

"Why would we do that? We can just make this child kill you all." The other girls all gasped and began to cry.

"I don't think you can, or you would have already. Yes, tonight would be awful, keeping Marie at bay with holy objects and herbs. We have a cross made of Rowan with us, so once the sun came up, we could either carry her upstairs into the sun or we could put the cross into her heart like a stake. Given a night or two to rest, I'm sure we could easily overpower your door, and while you rested the day away, we could drag each of you into the sunlight."

Damica looked around the room, knowing that there was no way any of these girls, except maybe Cassandra, would help her kill the monsters. But the monsters did not know that.

"Come out, and we can deal in person. I will not harm you."

Damica replied, "Your word then that no harm will come to me or any of the people on the ship tonight, no harm by anyone, not just you."

There was a soft chuckle from outside the door, "You are smarter than the rest, I see. My word, none of mine will harm any of yours tonight."

Damica was not satisfied with that. For one, none of these girls were hers. Another issue was what about the men above. For the past few nights, the girls had heard the men scream in agony as they were killed. Tonight, Damica wanted no death.

"No harm to any of the humans on this ship, not the girls in this room or the crew above. That is the stipulation for beginning the dealings.

"But how will we live? How will Marie live," whined the voice.

"Oh please," sighed Damica. "I know you can go the night without feeding. I also know that if Marie is so bad off and so important to you, you will feed her. It is one night we are working on, not years. Do we have an agreement?"

"Yes," said a pouty voice through the door. *Older than light*, thought Damica, *somehow I doubt that very much.* She moved herself toward the door. Marie moved as if she was being controlled.

"I will move the wards, then you tell Marie to open the door."

"I do not take orders from the likes of you," said the voice.

"Well, then, I guess we don't come out." Damica stood there calmly, breathing in and out in a rhythmic pattern the way her aunt had taught her to when in deep stress.

She counted up from one to see how long this stalemate would last. Finally, the voice agreed. Damica stepped closer to the door and moved the herbs in such a way as to create a larger circle on the outside of where the door would swing. The ward was thinner, but she figured it could work. As Marie stepped closer and opened the door, Damica moved the herbs to create a closed half-circle around the open door. *This should protect the others,* Damica thought as she straightened her back, lifted her head, and took a deep breath before stepping outside the room for the first time at night.

Chapter Nine

The woman that stood in front of her had blond hair and the lightest blue eyes she had ever seen, they had a rim of white around the outside of the iris with the blue that of the sky. They were almost inhuman. Damica was sure that these were the eyes this woman had had as a mortal; they were just unusual. The woman had Marie on her knees next to her, holding the back of her neck the way you would an unruly dog. Damica could not get a good gauge on her height as she was leaning slightly, but she could feel in her chest that this one was not nearly as old as she liked to play at.

"I need to speak to whoever is in charge, please," said Damica demurely, trying not to anger the woman.

"I am. You can call me Jeanne." She bowed her head slightly, but her eyes never left Marie.

"Really, we are going to play this? You are not in charge. There is no way the person in charge would put themselves in such a lowly position as to be checking on us. If you don't mind, I would really like to get this moving, so if you could call or think to or whatever you do to get the person in charge here, I would appreciate it."

Damica crossed her arms and tapped her foot in an impatient way. Jeanne looked down at her then as though she was the most interesting thing in the world. Those white-blue eyes were enough to send an invisible shiver down Damica's spine. She did not hold the gaze long. She knew better than to be bespelled by this thing. She may not be the oldest, and Damica was sure she was not the most powerful, but she was powerful enough to take hold of her. Damica thought *I will just play it safe and keep my gaze away from her eyes directly.*

"How dare you question me, human!" It came out as a roar. Damica was not phased. She knew that some vampires had the power of voice. They could instill fear or panic, bring sadness or lust with just their voice. She placed her hand on her tree amulet, closed her eyes, and let the power roll over her like water dripping off as she stepped out of a lake. When only the last few drips were left, she opened her eyes to see the woman staring at her. Marie was sprawled on the floor.

"Are we ready then?" She asked and picked up her skirts as though she was ready to go. The vampire just stared at Damica with her mouth pinched closed and her eyes full of venom, ready to spew poison. They would if they could.

"Fine, but keep up." She turned so fast that Damica did not even see her until she was ten feet ahead. She whispered a small prayer to her mother and followed the two vampires up the stairs.

Damica didn't know what to expect, but she was sure of one thing, she would not go all the way to the vampire's room if she could help it.

"I think we should have the meeting up here on the deck."

The vampire Jeanne turned and glanced at her with such an evil smile on her face, "Why, my dear, are you afraid?"

"Of course I am. Only a fool wouldn't be. More than that, negotiations should always be done on neutral territory. That's the way of it." She crossed her arms and stared at the vampire, making sure to never look beyond her nose. "Go fetch your master; see what they think. I am done speaking with a peon."

As she expected, this enraged Jeanne, she flung her arm out and Marie went flying. Damica could not tell if she had actually touched the girl or not. The vampire stormed toward Damica, breathing so hard spit flew from her mouth. Damica knew this could be her last moment; she looked directly into the woman's eyes with a bored expression and said, "No."

Such a simple word, but it stopped her in her tracks. She could not get any closer to Damica. She could move still, which meant Damica had underestimated her or had overestimated her own skill. That was something to be mulled about later. Jeanne let out a guttural scream, more like an animal than a human. Still, Damica waited. Her will would keep her safe, and hopefully, the right person or thing would hear all the commotion above and come to check it out. She didn't have to wait long, the purple dress of the dark woman she had seen on the dock and in her room was the first thing that caught her eye.

She was at least five foot ten with jet-black hair and eyes as dark as her soul. No, wait, they were dark but dark blue. Damica took a moment to realize that she was getting lost in those eyes and looked away, but not before she saw the little tilted smile on the woman's lips. She stepped before Damica, who had to look up and up to see her. She casually turned her head to Jeanne, "What are you going on about?"

Jeanne dropped to her knees before this woman and sniveled, "She demanded to see you. She disrespected my position as second, and she has this, this thing about her, so I cannot kill her." She put her head down at the woman's feet, "Please make it so I can kill her master."

"Thing about her, you say?" She put her hands out, and sure enough they were stopped about six inches from Damica's face. "Oh, that is nice! An egg shape, I believe."

She circled Damica, running her hands around the protections. It took all Damica had not to turn with the woman. She knew her ward would hold up to this type of touch. She also knew that this woman was old. She was the leader. The weight in her chest was immense; it wanted to drag her down under this woman's age. The things she must know, the power she must wield! Damica would do her best with her most potent weapons, her mouth and her mind, to try to stay alive. She wasn't sure any of her wards would be powerful enough to keep this one out if she didn't want to be.

"Why an egg shape?" asked the woman.

Damica stuttered a bit, "At my height, you could either reach in over the top, or I would be expending too much energy trying to get it up higher."

"Smart, I like this witch. That is what you are, I presume."

"Some say that. I just am what I am."

The woman smiled an actual genuine smile.

"I think you and I will get along famously, witch. Now what is it that you wanted to discuss?" She turned off the intensity like a switch and was now all business but in a relaxed way. The woman, Jeanne, was not so calm. She glared at Damica and hissed silently, letting her see her fangs. Damica raised her eyebrows but kept cool as she looked towards the taller woman.

"I would like to negotiate a peace treaty for the rest of the voyage. We have a few months or so left to get to New Orleans, and if I am correct, your girls do not need to feed for that time. Also, we will be stopping in Hispaniola first. If need be, you can get a sip there from a local."

The woman laughed long and deep. "Throwing the locals at us, are you? They may not be so happy with that if they knew." She smiled, contemplating Damica. "You could be my second, you know; you have much power. I can taste it." She stuck the tip of her tongue out of her mouth, between her teeth, and touched her top lip with it. Damica wasn't sure what to do with that. She kept silent and just stared at the woman.

"It seems as though you want everything, and we get nothing." She gave what Damica could only describe as a sultry pout.

"That is what we want. To make it safely to our destination," replied Damica, a bit out of sorts with the way this woman was outright flirting with her.

"So, we get nothing?" The pretty pout was still there. Damica wondered if this worked on many people. It left her uncomfortable and slightly out of sorts.

"What is it we can offer?" She asked.

"I want your name, and I want to be able to converse with you on a nightly basis. If you can do that, then we'll have ourselves a deal, witch."

There was a howl of outrage from Jeanne, "No! How will the rest of us live? She has dishonored me. I demand retribution!" The head vampire glared back at her and with just a look, brought blood pouring out of Jeanne's nose. Jeanne began to grovel and moan.

"You will not question me; you can feed off that new one if you must. Or if you want to keep her, you can feed her yourself. This is for me to decide and you to follow."

Damica could feel the power of her words wash around her protective egg. She could not imagine what it would be like to get the full brunt of that power, yet she felt as though this was not the extent of what this woman could do. She could feel the fear begin to bubble up. What was she getting herself into?

"Damica."

The woman turned her attention away from the other vampire.

"My name is Damica. Yes, I will agree to meet you every night until we get to Hispaniola. Then I would like time to rest and prepare for my new life."

The woman smiled radiantly with all that charm directed right at Damica, "Appolline, I look forward to speaking with you."

She turned and strode away, whistling a strange tune as she went. Jeanne and Marie followed, Jeanne still dripping blood as she went. Damica sighed, not sure what she was in for but knowing she could keep the rest safe, at least for a while.

Chapter Ten

The next night arrived, and there was a knock at the girls' door, "Appolline requests your presence."

Damica sighed; she was nervous. She had dressed in her second-best dress, done her hair as best she could without having washed it in a while, and had made sure she was clean. She put a bit of rose petal in her bodice, hoping it would work to make her smell presentable while also keeping the vampire at bay. She stepped out onto the deck; the stars were shimmering all around her. The men were nowhere to be seen, but she knew someone must be steering the ship.

By the edge of the ship, in a cleared-off section, was an elaborately set table with half a dozen lit candles sitting atop a beautiful tablecloth the color of the sky as the sun set right before the stars came out. It was set with an exquisite meal and, of course, Appolline sitting, waiting. Damica lifted her skirts just enough so she could hurry over.

She bowed ever so slightly to the vampire and took her seat, making sure to put up her shield to protect herself. "This is lovely, such a nice change from eating every meal within that room." She took a deep breath in; the salt air was mixed with the lovely scent of the food.

"Well, dear, you could always eat with me."

A zip of emotion shot through Damica, but she quickly pushed it aside. Tonight was about staying alive and in one piece. If she could make it through tonight, she felt as though she could make it through the rest of the journey.

She noticed there was only one plate. "Are you not eating?" she asked.

"Part of our curse is that we cannot eat food or drink wine. It tastes as though we are eating the ash from a fire pit. It does nothing for us nutritionally either, so why waste the energy."

She shrugged and looked slightly sad about this, "I miss good wine and better food. I miss pastries most of all. There is only so much that can be done on a ship, but I do hope you enjoy it." She said this as she took the top off a dish made up of fish and some small potatoes. Damica knew not much was left in storage but was very pleased to see the next plate revealed an orange.

"Oh, an orange, how lovely! Thank you for your thoughtfulness." She smiled genuinely at the vampire, almost forgetting not to look directly into her eyes. The vampire smiled back.

The evening was full of good conversation and some laughter. At no point did Damica forget that she was in danger, but she thought if this was the price to pay, it was not all that bad. They left each other right before dawn. Both expressing that they were looking forward to the following evening.

The evenings continued like this. Damica would be brought out on deck, there would be a table set, and the two women would talk long into the night about every topic imaginable. It got so that Damica looked forward to this ritual, though she never forgot her shields and never looked Appolline in the eyes.

It still seemed a small price to pay to keep everyone safe. No one had been hurt, or at least killed, since the deal had been struck. Damica was sure that no one had been used as food within the girls' room, but she could not guarantee that the crew had not been used for a sip here and there. On occasion, Jeanne could be seen watching them from the shadows. Damica could feel the hatred rolling off her, and she made sure never to be alone after dark, even on the way up and down from the deck.

As the nights went on, Appolline got more and more flirty. She was putting her hand out on the table as if to hold Damicas, who had her shields up so no one could touch her. The vampire would lean forward seductively as if to give her a view of her bosom. Damica was slightly uncomfortable with all this, she had never flirted with anyone, male or female, but she was pretty sure she was not interested in the vampire in that way.

She loved the conversation. Appolline had traveled all over the world and through all different time periods, which gave her lots of tales to tell.

She told of other extraordinaires she had met throughout the years, where they were, and what they could do. She told tales of fairies and goblins, giants and dwarves, as well as of people who Damica had never heard of.

She told of a great wall in the east where Appolline was fond of going to get silk, and of great pyramids farther south of Egypt, in an area that was not known for them. She kept Damica intrigued and entertained, and each morning she would write down what she had learned in her journal. This was the most exciting thing that had happened to Damica. Even the flirting excited her a bit.

Before they knew it, they were a day away from the stop at Hispaniola, effectively ending the evening get-togethers once the ship arrived, as they had agreed upon. As Damica dressed for the evening, she glanced around at the girls, feeling unsure of everything that had happened on this journey. They were all getting excited to see land, and hopefully, they would be able to see the blue sky tomorrow.

Damica did a quick survey of her supplies and took note of how empty they were. In fact, many of them had been used altogether. She was hoping to be able to refresh some of them on the island. She took one last look down at herself and was satisfied with how she looked, and she headed up to see Appolline one last evening.

The stars were brighter than usual, almost as if they knew it was the last evening. The breeze was soft and smelled of the familiar salt air. Appolline stood next to the table as Damica emerged. She held out her arms to Damica as if expecting a hug. Damica smiled but did not approach closer than was necessary.

"Oh, I thought this being our last night, I might get a hug."

"I'm sorry, I am not really a toucher. I enjoy your company, but I am not comfortable with that."

Appolline pouted prettily but sat without issue. The dinner was thin tonight, just some oatmeal and the ever-present orange, but Damica did not mind. She was content with the company and the stars; she was excited to see her new home in a few days.

"Damica, I know we have spent these last few months talking about everything under the moon and skies. I have kept my end of the bargain, as have you. I would hope that I have grown to mean something to you as you have to me."

Damica nodded and smiled. "I have enjoyed our time together very much. I have learned so much from you."

Appolline smiled back. She reached below the table and pulled out a small box. "I know you are going to New Orleans to get married and begin a new life. I have found that I do not want our conversations to end. Please consider this before you say no. I can offer you riches, travel, and immortality. It has been decades if not centuries, since I have found someone who piques my interest in life the way you do. I do not want to lose you. Please consider joining me for eternity."

She opened the box and pushed it towards Damica, revealing a beautiful emerald ring set in a bed of blue velvet.

Damica sat stunned for a moment. "I.. I'm sorry. That is not something I can do. I do not want immortality; I do not want to live only at night. I enjoy our conversations, but I do not feel that way about you. I'm sorry."

She got up from the table, aware that she may have brought the ire of the vampire down upon herself, but she wanted to see the sun again. As she walked back to her room, she could hear the echo of Jeanne's laughter ringing behind her.

Chapter Eleven

The sun rose, the girls would usually be settling in for some sleep, but the idea of seeing land for the first time in months kept them all awake and giddy. The crew were all in good spirits; no one wanted to bring up those who didn't make it to the island. Damica headed up to the deck with the other girls to catch the first sight of land.

The crew all took note of them and made a point to nod to Damica in thanks for the deal she had made to keep everyone safe. No one had died since she struck up her deal. As the ship docked, a cheer rose up from the girls and the crew. They all bustled to be the first ones off the ship, but the captain stood between them and their way off.

"Ladies, I wish you would stay aboard. This is not the cultured place you are used to. It is dirty and hot. The men are harsh, and the women are harsher. If you must go, please stay together and return before dark."

He looked at Damica intensely. He was aware of the deal she had made and knew that the population would not be safe while they were docked here. No one heeded him, and soon they were all en route off the ship and into the town. They agreed to stay together, all except Damica, who needed to find very specific items if she were to continue to keep everyone safe.

As they left the ship, most of the girls headed in one direction toward the market, and all the men headed another.

Damica walked with the girls until they reached their destination, then she moved off to look at things that no one else would be interested in.

As she walked through the streets, Damica could not get past the heat! She was sweating through her clothes. Not only was it hot here, but the dampness hung in the air. She had never felt air so heavy before. When she approached the part of the marketplace she wanted to visit, she was absconded by a small grey tiger cat who threw himself down in front of her. He rolled, demanding she rub his belly with a deep-throated meow. “Well, hello there little man. How is your day going?”

Damica had a soft spot for cats. Their farm always had a number of them about. She reached down and rubbed him on the belly and then on the head as he purred noisily. “I have no fish for you; in fact, I really need to be on my way if I am to make my purchases and be back before dark, have a good afternoon Monsieur Cat.”

She walked away into the marketplace. There were wares of all kinds, fresh fish and meats, as well as herbs and vegetables. Damica made her way past some colorful cloth and weaved through the crowd to the herb vendor. She was intrigued by the herbs, some familiar, some she had never seen. She knew what she needed them for but was leery of asking for their purpose. As she looked, she felt a small furry beast thread its way between her feet.

“Hello, Monsieur Cat. I see we have become fast friends.”

“Two,” said a masculine voice behind her. Not thinking they were talking to her, she continued her conversation with the cat.

“Two,” repeated the voice.

She looked up to see a stern-faced man of about twenty years standing behind her. He was dressed like a gentleman with skin that was the color of cafe au lait; his green eyes nearly glowed with intensity. Damica guessed him to be about six feet tall as she had to look way up to see him.

“His name is Two. He was the second born to the litter. Don’t let him sweet talk you into buying him anything. He is very well fed.”

Two ran up the man’s body and sat on his shoulder, glaring at him as if to say, *How dare you give me away! I was this close to getting a treat.*

Damica laughed out loud at the cat, then stopped short. It had been so long since she laughed. The last time was probably at something Marie had done. The thought saddened her, and she turned back to the table to look over the herbs a bit more. The man stood there behind her, not moving. She started to feel a bit uncomfortable and decided to move on to the next table.

"Excuse me." She said as she walked away.

The man followed her.

"May I help you find something?"

"I am searching for some herbs for my medicine bag." Damica blurted out. She wasn't sure why she said that. It wasn't something she was apt to tell anyone, but he put her out of sorts just enough that she kind of wanted to make him go away, so she was hoping to shock him enough for him to leave her be.

"What type exactly? I know a shop that has better herbs than here. I can show you."

He continued to stare at her until she let out a sigh and mentally scolded herself for being so uncomfortable. She had no idea what she was looking for here, only what kind it would have been in France. A little local help, carefully spoken to, would be needed for a while, she supposed.

"Dried rose for one, blackthorn, buckthorn, and holly or juniper are what I need for now." The man stood straight up, his eyes widening just a touch, and he let out a breath.

"You might find rose here but not dried. Come with me. I know a place that will have more of what you need. Those are some very specific herbs you mentioned. Not all of those can be found here, but I know a woman that will be able to help you."

He started to walk in the direction away from town when he realized Damica was not following, he turned and gestured with his hand. Two weaved his way between her ankles, then trotted off toward his master, stopping to look back at her as if to say, *it's okay, he's safe.* Damica sighed, still leery of following a stranger in a strange town. Still, the cat seemed confident in it, so Damica deemed she should be confident as well.

They walked for a time, Damica had caught up to him, and they walked side by side with the cat between them.

"Might I ask your name as we are going on this hike together? It seems only right that Two know who he is walking with," said the man. The cat let out a little chirp and looked up at Damica.

"My name is Damica, and you, sir? What should I call you?"

The way she worded the question made him laugh.

"Well, mademoiselle, I have been called many things in my life, none of which should be said by a lady, so you may call me René, René Colléte."

He stopped and bowed to her. This made Damica giggle a bit, "I am the bastard son of Claude Colléte, so you might want to be careful who sees you with me."

He stood up and smiled as he dramatically looked around them.

"Well, René, I will keep that in mind as we head to where we are going, which might be...." She left the sentence open, so he knew it was a question.

"To see my grandmother, she will know what you are needing. More so than any of the vendors in the market will. I am assuming you need protection from something. Grand'Mere will be able to help you out with that." Damica stood in stunned silence, watching René walk a few steps.

"How did you know? I mean, whatever could you mean?"

René chuckled, "When you meet Grand'Mere, you will understand. Come on, though, the captain will not wait for you, and you do not want to be out here at dark."

They walked a bit through the tropical landscape. Damica could not believe how hot it was here! She was dripping sweat by the time they arrived at the cabin in the jungle. It was a small one-room cabin made up of a mix of coquina and local wood, there was smoke coming from the chimney, but the inhabitant was sitting on an old rocking chair on the rickety front porch.

When she saw them approach, a smile broke across her wrinkled face. This was the oldest, darkest woman Damica had ever seen, René had lovely darker skin, but his Grand'Mere's was pitch as the darkest part of the night. She threw her arms around René and murmured things that Damica could not hear or understand in his ear, but she could tell they were said with love to her grandson.

"Grand'Mere, this is Damica. I do believe she needs some specific herbs that you might be better at getting her and making sure that she has the correct ones she needs. I believe she has traveled from France and will need some guidance in the herbs and remedies on this side of the Atlantic."

Damica nodded and curtsied to the old woman. The look the Grand'Mere gave her was stern.

"Do not curtsy to me, child. I am not of the standing to deserve that."

Damica was a little taken aback. Anyone in her world back in France who had knowledge and years was due respect.

"I... I'm sorry, madam. I was taught to respect my elders."

René smiled and squeezed his Grand'Mere's hand before looking at Damica.

"You will find on this side of the Atlantic that respect is often given to those whose skin is a different color. My Grand'Mere is still a slave to my father. My mother, herself, was a slave until her death. I am a free man of color only due to my father's generosity and his being given the chance to annoy his wife and son with my very existence."

His Grand'Mere patted his hand, "It's alright, René, you take your freedom and be a great man. Your mother would be so proud."

Damica felt as though she was trespassing on this personal moment and took a step backward.

"No, no, my dear, if René says you need help, I am here to help. What exactly are you needing, and what do you need it for?"

Grand'Mere stepped forward and placed a surprisingly strong hand on Damica to lead her back to the chairs, "René, there is something to drink in the kitchen, a little catnip tea to cleanse the blood. Please bring it out along with three glasses. We cannot have your guest being thirsty. She is not used to this climate, are you, my dear? No worries! We will get you all settled now, tell me what you need."

As they sat down, Grand'Mere looked at Damica with such intensity that there was a tiny spark between them. Damica knew right away that this was a woman she could trust, a woman who was the same as she was, a woman with knowledge and power even if her life situation told a different story.

"You are a healer, aren't you?" Damica stared at the woman, Grand'Mere chuckled with such a rich sound it comforted her more.

"In a sense, though, I do think we are different flavors of the same tea. Out with-it, girl. Why would you run so far from a ship that leaves very soon to get some herbs."

"Vampires." That one word made Grand'Mere sit back on her chair.

"New or old?" Damica was so relieved she could have cried.

"Both, there are some old ones, one new one made on the voyage and one very old one. We have struck a deal for safety, but I would like to replenish my stock before we land in New Orleans. I am unsure I will have time before whatever has been set in motion for my future begins."

René returned with the drinks at this moment, handing Damica a crude cup with the most delicious cold tea within.

"What have you been using to keep them at bay?" asked the old woman.

"Dried rose, buckthorn, hawthorn, and what I had of juniper as well as a rowan cross. Each night I am required to dine with the oldest one. I carry my charm, some rose, and I put up a boundary around myself."

The old woman smiled, "Good girl, clearly you are clever and powerful. You will need to be careful when you get to port. Those are not traits that are looked upon favorably for marriage." Damica frowned at the idea of marriage, but one problem at a time.

"I have some rose you can have, as well as some garlic, anything that is strong smelling they do not like. Once you get to New Orleans, you will have to learn quickly about what's around. You will have to find a way to use your power in a more direct fashion as well. There are many there that can teach you. Even if the flavor is different, they will be able to help." She got up and moved into the house, leaving René and Damica on the porch.

"So, you're going to be married," René said with a smirk.

"I suppose I was never consulted about this, so if I can get out of it, I will." Damica set her jaw in defiance. She was so caught up in her own anger that it took her a minute to notice that René was laughing.

"Are you laughing at me? This is not funny. Who in their right mind would travel across the world to marry someone they had never met? This is absurd!" She had stood up while speaking; her hands were clenched in fists at her side. It was at this moment that Grand'Mere returned with a small package of dried herbs.

"Is everything alright, dears?"

"Yes," said Damica, "we are fine." Though her scowl at René let him know that clearly, they were not fine.

"I have packed up some dried rose, as well as some catnip that will help you keep your blood clean should you need it. Also, what little sarsaparilla root I have left is in there, and some Quassia. All of these should help." She smiled kindly at Damica and took her face in her hands. "You stay safe, child. Keep those around you safe. You have some magic in you that I cannot touch, but if you need it, it will be there."

Damica was flustered by the intensity of the stare and the kindness of the old woman who had handed her a rather substantial package. René cleared his throat as the two women took this moment.

"We must be off if you are to make your ship before dark. Grand'Mere, I will be back as soon as I can." The old woman stepped away from Damica and hugged René fiercely.

"I know, child. Take care of yourself." The two smiled at each other, Damica could see the resemblance in their faces, but that was where it ended. One was a slave clothed in torn garments, while the other was dressed in the highest fashion. One dark as the night sky, one the warm coloring of a strong cup of tea.

The cat, Two, climbed Damicas dress so as not to be forgotten in all the emotion of the goodbye. She held him tight and tried not to cry.

Damica was sad to be leaving so soon. Grand'Mere reminded her so much of her family. René hurried them along the route back to the docks, the small argument of earlier forgotten. The cat stayed perched in Damicas arms for part of the trip but moved onto her shoulder for the rest. He was quite content with himself, purring so loud there was no way conversation would have been permitted.

As they neared the ship, Damica reached up to pet Two, "You should probably take your cat back before he follows me onto the ship." René lifted his arms, and the cat sprang into them. "Thank you for introducing me to your Grand'Mere. I am so grateful to have someone that understood what I needed." They stood awkwardly for a moment.

"I'm sorry I upset you by mentioning the marriage. It's just that...." He trailed off just as the captain walked past, mumbling to Damica that she best get her arse on the ship before they decided to leave.

Without thinking, Damica went up on tiptoes and kissed René on the cheek. "Thank you for everything. If you are ever in New Orleans, find me."

Part Two: New Orleans

Chapter Twelve

That night was quiet. The girls and crew all knew that the only reason they had peace was because someone on land did not. They accepted this and slept through the night. The ship left port the next day at about high noon. The girls napped and gossiped about their trips to town and dreamt of their futures that were so close at hand. When Damica had unwrapped the herbs that Grand' Mere had packed for her, she found a book full of remedies and protective potions the old leaf doctor had snuck in. She had also noticed what she could only think of as spells within the book.

She was sad and lonely thinking that Grand'Mere had sent her on her way with probably her most prized possession. If she ever ran into René again, she would make sure to send it back. Though she was glad to have it and happy to see a bit of her old life carry over into her new life. She happily compared her family's books with the new one, seeing what remedies overlapped and what ones were new.

The knock on the door came at sundown, just like it always did. Damica was surprised as the deal only went until they landed on Hispaniola. She was willing to do what needed to be done to keep everyone safe, even if it meant spending more time with the vampire. She straightened her skirt, put up her shield of protection, and walked up to meet Appolline.

The vampire was dressed so extravagantly that she made Damica feel like a street urchin in her dirty dress that she had worn on her hike the day before. Laundry was not something that was easily done on a ship. Her hair was unwashed and just thrown up in a bun, and she did not have time to put any color on her face. Damica was not really bothered by this. She was used to not quite looking the part of the lady. The memory of home made her smile, and she was lost in thought as she approached the table.

"What is on your mind, my love? You don't seem to be here at all, even though it is our last night to ever be together. I know this wasn't part of the deal, but I was hoping that you would want to see me as much as I wanted to see you," pouted Appolline.

"I'm sorry, it's been a long couple of days, and I am tired. What was it you were saying?"

Appolline giggled like a schoolgirl. She was doing her best to engage Damica with stories. She was tilting her head from side to side and using her arms to make her cleavage appear larger.

Appolline tried to touch her several times through the barrier but would pull her hand away and twirl her hair in such a way as to look demure and alluring.

Damica tried to pay attention, but her mind was on her books, and she kept feeling this movement around her feet. Glancing down, she was shocked to see Two weaving between her feet.

"Two! How did you get here?" She scooped the cat up and snuggled it close.

"What is that thing?" Screeched Appolline just as Two hissed and launched himself at the vampire.

"Two, No!! Bad kitty." But it was too late. The cat had the vampire pinned to the deck of the ship. She was screaming as Damica unattached each claw individually from her dress.

"How dare you bring that beast here! Jeanne, take that thing and throw it overboard!"

Jeanne started forward with an evil grin, but she seemed to forget that Damica had a bubble of protection around her that now protected the cat in her arms. She tried to grab the cat but was met with not only a wall of energy but a shock from it as well. It was powerful enough to knock her back. She hissed at Damica at the same time Two hissed at her. He then climbed up on Damicas shoulder and began to clean himself as if neither of the vampires were really worth his time.

"I'm sorry, Appolline, maybe we should just call it a night, I am tired, and it seems Two is ready for bed as well" Damica backed slowly away from the two vampires still sitting on the deck of the ship. When she got within a foot or so of the stairs, she turned and ran into her room.

When the boat docked the following day, all the girls were ready to start their new lives, well Damica was just ready to be done with the ship. She grabbed her *cassette* of belongings, the small bag of herbs, along with the books Grand'Mere and her mother had given her, made sure the cat was secured on her shoulder, and headed off to the dock. The sun was shining, the air was thick with people, dirt, and humidity.

When the girls exited the ship, a small crowd of people was there to see them. Who were these women that had come all this way to marry some of them? The people openly stared at them, whispering and pointing. The men seemed dirty and rough, there were a few dressed as gentlemen within the crowd, but for the most part, this crowd was not what was promised to the girls. Of course, nothing about this trip so far was what was promised.

It had been so long since most of the girls had seen the sun, and the New Orleans weather was hot and humid, the air so damp it felt heavy to them. Many of the girls immediately hid their eyes, their fair skin turning red, not so much from the sun as the heat and humidity combined with all the layers of clothes that they wore.

They all dripped sweat, rolling down their faces and necks, puddling in their armpits and bosoms. Not the best first impression. Soon there was a murmuring from the crowd. Just as the girls were beginning to feel unwelcome as well as physically uncomfortable, the crowd parted to let the local nuns approach.

They were all lined up with their hands in praying position and their heads down. It seemed like a parade through the dirt and mud. Damica had never been so happy to see nuns in her life. They broke through the crowd just as one of the girls fainted.

The crowd burst into noise, the murmur now a roar. Damica and the other girls rushed to the body on the ground, fanning her as best they could.

As Damica picked her head up, she called out, "Water, does anyone have any water."

Not a soul moved toward them. Even the nuns had stopped in their tracks. Damica had carried Two with her off the boat, he had quietly slipped away as the crowd had gotten bigger, but he now made his way through the legs of that same crowd with a child in tow. He ran to Damica, the child right behind, carrying a cup of water.

"Thank you, thank you so much. Both of you." Damica tilted the girl's head and gently poured some water into her mouth.

The girl's eyes fluttered open dramatically, "No, not you! Not you!" The girl screeched.

It was not the reaction Damica expected, maybe not undying gratitude but definitely not the revulsion she saw in the girl's eyes.

"I'll take her," said Cassandra, "Not all the girls were okay with your deal with...." She left the word unsaid. She had whispered the rest of the sentence. No one wanted the locals to know what they had traveled with.

Damica felt as though she had been slapped in the face. All she had done to keep them safe, yet still, some were afraid of her. Some were more afraid of her than they were when they had found she was a healer. She stepped back, a little lost as to what to do. Just then, Two decided to get her attention with a sharp brrrb. She looked down as he rubbed his thank you to the child, then jumped up on Damicas dress and climbed her to sit on her shoulder. The murmur of the crowd, which had gotten quiet, began again.

"That cat, where did it come from? Did you see that? She must be a witch." Words like these were swirling around her. Two head-butted her to get her attention just as the nuns broke their reverie and began to move forward to gather the girls.

"Ladies, I am Mother Superior. Please gather your belongings and follow me. We will be headed down to the west end. We have a temporary shelter there until our nunnery is built. Come along."

The Mother Superior did not hesitate as she ushered all the girls ahead of her, making sure they turned left down the street. The rest of the nuns gathered around the girl who had passed out. They hailed a passing cart and escorted her on board. One nun stayed with her; the rest took up position behind the girls.

"I thought there would be more of you," said Mother Superior. None of the girls wanted to tell her there were more. They had lost two or three to death, and the rest were still asleep on the ship, and they would not awaken until dusk.

The walk was invigorating as well as exhausting at the same time. For two months, these girls had been shut in a cabin within a ship, only allowed out on deck for a few minutes each day. It felt good to stretch their legs, but not having done so in such a long time, combined with the incredible heat and humidity, made many of them stumble as if drunk. They were exhausted from lack of sleep. Fear of their situation on the ship had kept them in a mindset of always being aware and never fully relaxing.

As they set eyes on the building, the large house that would be their home for the next few days, at the very least, a collective sigh went through the group. Vampires could not come into holy spaces, right? They could all finally relax and sleep, eat a good hot meal, and be excited for the prospects to come.

Damica smiled a little, still unsure of how she was going to get out of marrying, but she was happy to see the other girls starting to relax. Two had ridden the whole way on her shoulder, sitting up as straight as he could. When they arrived at the door, the Mother Superior gave the cat a glare, then looked at Damica in such a way that she knew this was not going to be a pleasant few days.

The girls were taken into the back and given a large room to share. There were plenty of cots and what seemed like a lot of space to air out all their clothes that had sat in the *cassettes* for two months. There was chatter and laughter again, just like that first night on the ship. Damica sat quietly by herself. Marie was not there to chatter her ear off or to try to get her to engage with the other girls.

This was the first time since she had been turned that Damica had a moment to mourn the loss of her friend. Tears rolled down her cheeks as she sat there listening to the girls. Two had hopped down from her shoulder to explore the room, but as soon as she started to cry, the cat jumped up on her lap to try to comfort her.

"Ladies," the Mother Superior walked in and around the room; she stopped a second and looked at Damica, then turned back to the room, "We will rest tonight. Tomorrow we will explore New Orleans. It is such a wonderful city, with so much potential. While we trek, you will get to see what you will be expected to do. You are here to help get the men settled, start a new generation, and to prosper in the Lord's name. Tomorrow night we will host a gathering for any men who have been granted permission to take a wife. I expect you to be on your best behavior. And maybe you might want to leave the cat behind."

She looked straight at Damica as she said this. Two was having none of it and sat with his leg up, cleaning himself and showing off that he was, indeed, a tom cat.

"Humph," said the mother superior as she took her leave of the room. When the door was closed, the girls burst out laughing, telling Two he was such a good kitty and trying to find small toys for him to play with. Damica laughed and smiled along with the other girls. Still, she didn't feel quite like she was welcome in their ranks, not like it had when Marie had dragged her into games of quadrille or to share funny stories. She did not even realize how much the girl had impacted her life and how she had been looking forward to continuing that friendship in this unfamiliar place until now.

The evening passed in relative peace and quiet. The girls began to get giddy with excitement at being in a new place. The food they were given was amazing. Fresh seafood and vegetables from the garden in a stew with herbs they had never tasted before. The night air was full of the buzzing of insects, the croaking of the frogs, and the smell of jasmine from the local gardens.

Damica had stepped out into the private garden the nuns worked for vegetables and herbs when she heard someone calling her name. The sun had just set, and the cacophony of sounds from the frogs, crickets, and mosquitos was almost deafening. It took her a moment to realize that it was not her imagination. There really was someone standing outside the garden calling her name.

"Mademoiselle Damica, is that you?"

"Who is asking?" She called out in a clear, bold voice

"Appolline sent me. She would like you to have this note. Might I come in and give it to you?" Not knowing if the delivery person was a vampire or not, Damica was not about to invite them into the garden of the nun's home.

"I don't know who you are, and I am in a new country, let alone city. I would prefer it if you place it on the ground and walk away. If you please, that will be the only way I will take the note."

"I was told to make sure it got into your hands; I do not find that acceptable."

"Well, then you can return to Appolline with the note still on your person. I am not so curious about its contents to bend on this. Either you leave it there or you take it back. That is your choice."

There was a long moment of silence, then a quiet voice came back, "I will leave the note here. May I watch that you get it? That way, I can say I saw it enter your hand."

"That will be fine. I will give you three minutes to leave it and get into a good spot. If you approach me, I will..." Damica was not sure what she would do, kill? Harm?

"Okay, mademoiselle, I understand. I am setting it down now."

Damica waited approximately three minutes, counting to one hundred and eighty slowly, then stepped outside the garden. There was no fence around the area, just higher plants delineating the end of the property. Right on the other side of the plants was an envelope with her name dramatically scrawled across one side. The paper had been sealed with a wax imprint of the letter A. She turned it around in her hands, not really wanting to open it. She sighed and walked back into the garden to find a seat and read her note, reminding herself that she needed to send her mother a letter as soon as possible.

My Dearest Damica,

I hope this note finds you well. I was despondent this evening when I realized that you had not waited for me or left me any sort of communication. I am sorry that our dinner last evening was disturbed by that cat. I do not have a fondness for felines. I am missing your beautiful face and your quick wit. I am looking forward to continuing our acquaintance.

Yours forever

Appolline

Damica sighed. She had hoped against hope that the vampire would just leave her alone after they had landed. It seemed as though she wanted to keep up the communication. Damica sat for a while in the evening until the mosquitos chased her inside, where her skin had been exposed was now covered in red, itchy bumps. She would normally have made herself a poultice of some sort to quell the itching but thought between the cat who loved to sit on her shoulder and the nighttime note she had just received, that maybe practicing healing in the home of the nuns was pushing her luck a bit for one day. She dressed in her night clothes and tried to settle in and sleep. Two curled right next to her while she tried to not scratch herself to the point of bleeding.

Chapter Thirteen

The day dawned with so much color in the sky it looked to Damica as though the sky had been painted. The jasmine and bougainvillea competed with each other in making the air smell sweeter than the bakery back in Toulon. With the beauty and wonderful scents, Damica felt as though she were in paradise, at least until she walked out of the cool building into the heat and humidity of the city.

The girls were woken up early, told to dress comfortably, and fed dark coffee and fresh bread with eggs from the nunnery's chickens. They were then given some chores to help with, from collecting the eggs to harvesting some fresh vegetables from the garden. A few of the girls were put to cleaning the kitchen. As the sun rose in the sky, the nuns soon gathered the girls to go for their walk around town.

They headed east along the river front until they reached the Place De Armes, then headed north up the Rue St Pierre until they got to where the church sat. They paused there momentarily before heading out into the town to meet some girls who had come before them.

There were small homes throughout the area, with beautiful gardens full of vegetables and some of the most amazing flowers the girls had ever seen. Most of the plants that were growing here were not anything like what they had seen in France. Damica knew she was going to have to learn new ways to keep her medical herbs full. She was fairly certain that many of her old standbys would not be easily found here.

As the girls walked, Two decided to explore. Damica was not sure whether to let him go or try to hold on to him, but he had found her on the ship, so she concluded that he would find her again. Occasionally, she would catch a peek of him up ahead or within some bushes harassing some birds. She found it refreshing to walk out in the sun, even if it was boiling hot. She did feel very alone without the little cat, who she had only known for a few days.

They toured two homes of what the nuns called "successful women" who had come from France to marry here. From what Damica could see, they did not seem very happy. There were multiple children at each home, and the women worked nonstop to harvest, clean, and care for the children. There were no men in sight to help, not that they would have. All of the work they were doing was considered women's work.

Damica was not happy at all about her prospects and thought again that she needed to find a way out of this. By the time they arrived back at the house, they had just a few hours to freshen up and get ready to go meet the men that were given permission from the king to marry a wife.

As the rest of the girls hurried around washing up and putting on their best dresses, doing their hair and makeup, Damica found her favorite black frock and put it on. It was flattering, but only because it fit her just right. At her height and being so tiny in the waist, sometimes dresses were hard to get made just the way she wanted them. Being exhausted from the long trip, the black color of the dress did no favors to her complexion, making her appear more drawn and washed out. She pulled her hair back in a severe bun and applied no makeup. *Well, hopefully this will help to deter anyone that would want to talk with me. I need to ask what happens to unmarried girls tomorrow*, she thought.

As the girls walked back through the city, the sun was just setting, the colors of the evening were more amazing than the dawn. The sky was a myriad of reds and pinks with a splash of orange and purple mixed in. Damica could not take her eyes off the sky as she walked. That is until she tripped over Two, who had found his way back to her after his adventures in the city that day.

"Well, hello, Two. I see you have decided to join me in this hell I am about to undertake. At least I have you to keep me company."

She smiled as the cat climbed up her and sat on her shoulder. When they entered the hall that had been set aside for this meeting, there was a murmur about the crowd. All eyes were on the girls as they walked in, Damica was not shy in the least, but all of this attention made her uncomfortable. She could not imagine what the other girls were feeling.

Of course, she was striding in, dressed in all black, with a cat on her shoulder which automatically meant that she was being stared at. The thought made her giggle, then laugh. As she tried to control the laughter, tears ran down her face. She wiped them away as best she could, but bursts of laughter kept overcoming her.

She looked at the other girls, who seemed horrified by her, which made her laugh harder. At least until she saw the face of the Mother Superior. The disapproval did not make her humor go away, but she understood that this was not the time or the place, so she got herself under control.

She looked out into the crowd; it had not hit her how many people actually were there until this moment. It was as if the whole city had come! Men and women alike were milling about and staring. They were all staring. One man in particular seemed to be staring right at Damica.

She quickly looked away as the nuns started the ceremony of introduction. At this time, the girls were supposed to mingle and hopefully meet the man of their dreams, or at least the man that would have them. Damica stayed where she was, Two still perched on her shoulder. Hoping against hope that no one would approach her, but of course, when women were not a normal thing to have around, they would approach any of them, even ones that were projecting to be left alone.

The first man that approached her was nice enough. He worked as an apprentice in a shop on the riverfront. Damica didn't pay much attention to what he was saying. She was too overwhelmed by the smell of fish that permeated his clothing. At least, she hoped it was his clothing that smelled so bad.

Her eyes began to water as she stood there with a fake smile plastered on her face, nodding away at whatever he was saying. Two, still perched on her shoulder, began to sneeze. Not the cute little cat sneezes but big wet sneezes that almost knocked him down. He seemed to spray the man with cat snot all over the side of his face. Damica could not remember when he had gotten so close to her as to be in the trajectory zone of cat sneeze, but she was grateful for Two's interference. She had no idea what she had been nodding at.

"Oh, my goodness, I am so sorry. Let me take my cat away. He seems to have an allergy to you. Have a nice night; it was nice to meet you." She smiled at the man as she walked away, then shook her head as she glanced at Two, who seemed quite pleased with himself.

The next man that approached her was the man she had noticed staring at her. When he introduced himself, his voice seemed eerily familiar. He took her hand and laid a kiss upon it, leaving a wet spot that Damica really wanted to wipe off on her dress, but she didn't. Her mother had taught her better than that, though she felt she should get a prize for not wiping it away.

He began to tell her all about himself and how his home could take care of her in the lap of luxury, that she would never want for anything. How his boss would ensure she had everything she could ever need, and how she was looking forward to seeing Damica.

Damica paused at that, "Your boss is looking forward to seeing me?"

"Why yes, mademoiselle, you are all she can talk about. Of course, she could not come herself after her long journey. And well, being a woman, she was not granted permission to marry one of you." He laughed at his own joke as Damicas blood ran cold.

"Might I ask who your boss is?" though she was pretty sure she knew the answer.

"Why mademoiselle, it's Appolline of course. I spoke with you last night, you made me leave the letter outside the garden. She was so pleased when you accepted it."

Damicas smile froze on her face. She was stunned that the vampire would want to continue their relationship even here. Two felt the difference in her body language and growled, then abruptly turned on her shoulder, unbalancing her as he jumped into the shoulder of another man that had approached from behind her.

"Two! How, what...."

Damica looked over her shoulder and started to laugh at René holding and snuggling the cat he thought was left behind on the island.

"René! I found him on the ship after we had left. I was hoping I would see you again. I don't want you to think I stole your cat."

René smiled back at her, his green eyes shining, his dark skin in contrast to the rest of the crowd around them. Damica was so relieved to see him that she did not see the look of rage come over the other man or the looks of disdain from any of the other men.

"Two has a mind of his own. If he was on the ship, it was his own doing."

His smile lit up the room. Damica found she could only keep her eyes on him.

"I see you are dressed to find a husband." The twinkle in his eye let her know he was joking and that he recognized what she was trying to do.

"Well, I thought it would deter people, but it seems to not be working. How are you here?"

"My father has decided I am to take a wife. Whether it's a real desire, which I doubt, or a way to make my life miserable while pissing people off, I am not sure."

"Oh, have you met anyone you would take?" They both turned and looked at the crowd, only then noticing Appolline's man had not left. "Oh, I'm sorry I never got your name. This is my friend René."

"Yes, I am aware of who he is," turning towards René, "the likes of you should not be allowed to marry one of these clean women."

René's face turned to stone, "Oh, I am sure that is the consensus but, alas, the king and my father believe otherwise. Don't you have someplace to be, someone to toady up to, eh Charles?" Damica was surprised they knew each other.

"Mademoiselle Damica," Charles said, trying to take her hand to kiss it again, "I will be by tomorrow with our offer."

Two let out a howl and jumped back to Damica, pushing her back with his weight. Charles drew his hand back and scowled at the cat.

"It was nice to meet you. Maybe we will see each other around."

Damica hoped that her words and tone would be taken as a dismissal. They both watched Charles walk away, then turned their attention back to the room.

"So, which young lady is striking your fancy? Maybe I can introduce you to them."

René tried to look seriously at all the contenders but just sighed, "I am the wrong color for any of these women to want to be married to. This is ridiculous that my father, and the king, would even think of making me do this. The only one that would have me would be one that was rejected by everyone else."

Damica took a long look at René. Between the beautiful green eyes, the latte-colored skin, the well-built physique, and his height, he must have been close to six foot, but of course, when you were as demure as Damica, everyone looked tall, she could not fathom why anyone would turn him down. And on top of all that, he came from a well-to-do family. He was a catch in her eyes.

"I'm sure it's not that bad, you aren't really that horrible looking, and you do kind of have a personality. I'm sure we can find someone that would have you."

René let out a whoop of laughter at her words that stopped all other noise around them. As he doubled over, she could see tears coming from his eyes.

"I'm sorry, was that cruel?"

"No, no, no, that is exactly what I needed." He stood up, took a handkerchief out of his pocket, and wiped his face, but he could not stop grinning.

Around them, the other people in the building seemed to find interest in them. Damica was suddenly uncomfortable. It seemed as if every eye in the place was on them. The cat had made its way back up on Damicas shoulder at some point, and she could only imagine the image that they made. Her, tiny, dressed all in black with a cat on her shoulder, and René, good-looking, laughing until he was in tears with skin darker than everyone else in the room. Yeah, they were a sight.

"I think I'm done looking for a husband tonight, René, it was nice to see you again. I hope to see you soon." She meant it. This man that could laugh at her was someone she would like to get to know more. "Would you like your cat back?"

René looked on the verge of laughter again, "No, I believe he has chosen you as his mistress. Might I walk you back to where you are staying? I don't mean to sound, well, like a man, but as a woman, it may not be safe to walk the streets alone tonight."

Damica thought about it for half a second, then nodded. She approached the Mother Superior to let her know she was not feeling well and would be headed back. The nun was not pleased but agreed to let her walk home if she had someone walk with her. Damica let her know she did, though she did not let her know it was René. In fact, she might have indicated that it was another girl. No need to correct the assumption.

Chapter Fourteen

The night was humid. Damica thought it felt like a warm blanket engulfing her as she walked. There were a few lights around, but for the most part, the night was dark. The crickets and the bullfrogs were making their own music, though it seemed to be out of sync a bit. The smells of the river were all around them as they walked in companionable silence, both lost in their own thoughts.

Damica noticed the air around them change. She couldn't pinpoint what it was exactly, just that there was a change. René looked up at the same time she did; there in front of them were Appolline, Jeanne, and Charles. René stepped forward and muttered something under his breath just as Damica wrapped her shields around herself and the cat. She looked over to see if she could possibly extend it to René, only to see a green glow around him.

"I see you are one that serves the spirits, sir. Alas, I am not sure why that would be of importance to me. I am just here to gather what is mine. Damica, come child. It is time to go home."

Appolline gave her companion a dismissive look while putting her hand out in a welcoming gesture. Damica could feel a slight tug within herself but quickly strengthened her shield and pulled out her necklace.

"That won't be necessary anymore, child. You know where you belong."

The tug got stronger just as Damica's necklace began to burn red hot. Just at that moment, a ball of energy came from René's direction aimed right at the trio. Charles flew back twenty feet or so. Jeanne screamed and flew to the side. Even Appolline got knocked aside.

"She does not wish to go; I will not allow you to force her!"

He stepped in front of Damica, forcing both their energies to blend, creating a purple light. Two jumped down and seemed to add his own little ball of power to the shield. Damica stepped up next to René to hold off the vampires together. He glanced over at her then his jaw dropped as he noticed the color change and the uniting of the shields.

"I think we may have more in common than just our love of the cat," he said to her just as Appolline threw her energy at them. It bounced off their wall of power.

"Jeanne!" she shrieked. "Bring her to me! I don't care what happens to him. I want her power!"

Jeanne flew forward at such speed that Damica was not even sure she saw a body flying toward them, just light and air. Just as she got within reach, Two spread out on the ground, looking as though he was so bored he just had to let out a stretch, only to have his back feet touch Damica while his front paws touched René. This set off such a power surge that Jeanne was thrown to the ground, her body smoking from where it had touched the power.

"I am not going with you, Appolline! The deal was while we were on the ship, I would spend time with you. We are done. No more!" The last word came out more as a roar than a word.

Appolline snarled at the pair, "You will be mine one way or another. I will possess you!"

Two broke the barrier at that moment and rushed at the vampire, growling and hissing, still covered in the purple light. He hit her right smack in the chest. She swatted him away. Where he had hit left a burned spot on the vampire. She grabbed Jeanne and sneered at Charles, then lifted up into the air and flew away. In a second, they were gone. Damica rushed over to find Two. He was on his side against some bushes where he had landed.

"Oh, Two, you saved us!" She said as she picked the purring cat up and snuggled him in her arms.

"Oh yes, it was totally the cat that saved us. Nothing to do with our own powers or the merging of them or how quick-witted I am," said René as he rolled his eyes. Two blinked at him from over Damica's shoulder as if to say, *of course, it was all me, you mere human*, then he snuggled into Damica's neck with a smug look on his face.

"Oh, you know what I mean. He launched himself at her! He drove her away!"

She hugged the cat closely, partly for the cat but mostly for herself. She wasn't quite sure what had just happened. Oh, she knew a vampire had tried to claim her. It was more the shields and the merging and René. What had she meant by "serve the spirits"? Damica was rattled and ready to go home.

"I think I am going to go the rest of the way alone. I'm not quite sure what we just did."

"The hell you are! I will walk the rest of the way to ensure you and the cat make it safe."

They walked the last few blocks in silence. When they got to the house, René walked to the door with her and held it open.

"Stay in tonight. Keep your amulet and that cat with you. You should be safe in here; I do believe it is holy ground and blessed. I will see you tomorrow, Damica." He turned and strode off into the shadows.

Still holding on to the cat, Damica made her way to her bed and started gathering her wits about herself. She thought she would never sleep, but the use of power had drained her so much that when the other girls came in, they found her curled on her bed, fully dressed, the cat sleeping on top of her.

Chapter Fifteen

The day dawned hot, the girls worked in the gardens as gentlemen came calling asking to speak with particular girls they had met the night before. Some left immediately, some had multiple suitors, and a few decided to wait and see.

Damica did not expect to get a suiter, so she was slightly peeved when she was called in. Had she not dressed as awfully as she could and made a point to be as rude and unappealing as possible? Of course, the caller was Charles, still trying to woo her for Appolline. As she entered the room, Two was right there beside her. Damica rolled her eyes and let out an audible sigh just as Two growled.

"Mademoiselle Damica, I am hoping to make an offer for you."

Charles had bruising around his temple where he must have hit his head during the fight, his eyes were swollen as if he did not have enough sleep or had been crying, and his shoulders were hunched. He did not look well. He looked as if he had been beaten, which perhaps he had been.

"No need, Mother Superior, I reject this suiter." She then turned to leave just as Charles threw himself at her feet.

"Please, madame, she means to kill me if I do not procure you. Please don't let me die."

Damica glanced down at him and shook his hand off her leg, "You wish me to perish instead? The answer is no. The answer will always be no. Go back and tell your mistress that."

Two lifted his tail straight up and walked past Charles as they left the room. A short while later, she was called back into the office, but when she entered, there was no gentleman to be seen, just the head nun.

"You know, Damica, you really should have taken that man's offer. A witch such as yourself, who flaunts it with your familiar and everything, should be grateful for any attention. Don't think I don't know what went on in that ship."

Damica thought for a moment before she answered, "I am not just any man or woman's toy, and I am most certainly not going to go with that man. If, as you say, you know what happened on the ship, then you would not have brought me down here for this. You may call me a witch, it would not be the first time someone has, but there are worse things here than I. Now if you will excuse me, I am going back to my bed for a rest. The heat is not something I am used to. Good day."

"I am not through with you yet, young lady. You do not dismiss me in my own house. I will see you burned at the stake the way the old country would do it! Oh, I can wait, you will see. Once no one marries you, and you reject all of them, it will not be difficult to convince them that you are a witch. They already think you are all vampires! As if such a thing could exist!"

Damica slid her eyes to the nun, there was a sly smile on her face, and Damica knew. She knew that this woman would try to burn her, she knew that all the work her mother went through to try to keep her safe from the witch-burning might be for nothing, and she knew, she knew that this woman was well aware that there were vampires about and that she was somehow connected to them. Damica suddenly hit with the notion that she would need to get away from here. The faster, the better. She was hustling out of the house with her head down when she ran right into the chest of René.

"Oh, I'm so sorry I didn't see you there."

"I guessed that when you barreled into me, it's funny, though, that the cat had stopped walking and didn't hit me. Here I thought you two shared a brain or something."

The look that Damica gave him would have wilted a lesser man, but it just made René smile more.

"You are just who I was hoping to see. I need to show you something that showed up at my door today." He took out a piece of paper that looked so old the edges were torn and yellowed. It stated quite simply, *She is mine, do not intervene again, or there will be consequences.*

"Oh yes, Charles made his way here already to try to marry me." She looked over her shoulder at the door she had just come from, "I think we might need to walk a bit if we are to talk. There are more ears here than there should be."

They walked a block or so away from the house without speaking, down by deep, brown river filled with ships moving along it.

"He begged me to go with him, said she would kill him if I did not come."

"I'm guessing you still said no?"

"Oh yes, I am sure I will be the one to die if I go or to not die. I am not fully sure of what she wants me for."

"After seeing your power last night, I am quite positive about what she wants you for. I think you are more than just a leaf doctor. I believe you have the touch. I think if Appolline were to make you a vampire, you would be beyond powerful. I think this is what she wants to do."

Damica scoffed, "I can put up a shield, and I can work relief with plants. That is the extent of my 'powers'"

"Nope, after seeing our energies merge, there is more there. You just have to learn how to work it. That's why I was coming to see you today. I have a proposition for you. Marry me, but not in the sense of a common marriage, just in name only. That solves both our main issues, I need to marry to keep my father happy, and you need to marry so you are, well, I'm not sure what would happen if you did not marry."

"Mother Superior has said she will make sure that I will be burned at the stake as a witch."

"Pleasant, godly woman, I see." René could not keep a shiver from passing through his body. "So, you see, it's in both our best interests. My home is big enough that if you never want to see me, that can happen. You can have one side of the house, and I will keep to the other. Is it a deal?"

He held out his hand for her to shake it. She looked at his hand skeptically but sighed and shook it. It seemed that she was going to be married after all.

Chapter Sixteen

The deal was done with very little fanfare. The Mother Superior was not pleased, to say the least. It seemed that Damica was a witch who was now going to marry an abomination. Both René and Damica found this highly amusing and had trouble not laughing as the paperwork was getting done. They gathered up Damicas belongings along with the cat, of course, then headed out to René's home east of the city.

The trek was bumpy and uncomfortable for more than just the ruts in the road. Though the carriage was beautiful. The driver was an older black gentleman who smiled delightedly at Damica as he helped her up.

Damica was unsure what to expect and hoped that René would keep his word about the marriage being just in word. As they turned into the drive to the house, she was stunned by the size of the plantation. The house itself was the largest structure, besides churches, that she had ever seen! With columns across the front and a wide porch dotted with chairs and tables, it was welcoming and grand simultaneously. The house itself was a beautiful shade of blue, so light in color that, at the wrong angle, it almost looked white. There were people scattered across the landscape as well, working in fields and sweeping that great porch.

"They are not all related to me, though some are. I am not legally allowed to give them their freedom until my father passes, so until then, I will try to be the best boss I can be. I give them livable conditions and good food. I keep families together and make sure that they do not overwork in the heat. I have to keep the plantation going, but I will not do it with the blood of these people. I do my best for them." This last part was said in a whisper.

Damica looked away from him, back at the beautiful scenery. She noticed a big tree with bottles hanging from it right outside the entrance to the house. She glanced back to ask about it but stopped when it was clear René was still in his head over the atrocity he was forced to live with.

As they pulled up to the entrance of the house, a lovely young lady ran out to open the door for them. Damica stepped out and was engulfed in the biggest hug she could imagine.

"Damica, this is my sister, Angelica. She is a little excited to meet you if you can't tell," René chuckled. The girl smiled down at Damica.

"René said I would like you, and I can just feel how much we are going to be friends. Let me help you to your room. We have set up the whole right wing for you. That way, you don't have to see my icky brother if you don't want to," though she was smiling and winking the whole time she said this.

The house was just as gorgeous inside as it was outside. The rooms that Angelica led Damica to were beautifully set, with a large bed and desk attached to a small sitting room. They were decorated in light blue with a touch of green, and the French doors opened up to the second-story balcony that looked out over an enchanting marshland. Angelica threw the doors open and let in the breeze. There was a storm brewing on the horizon. Damica was so taken aback by the accommodations she was speechless.

"I know it's fancy, right? When they first sent me here from the main house, I thought it would be lesser somehow, but it's amazing! I love it here. And René is good to me." She smiled sadly, "He is trying to get the rest of the family here, but father will not allow it."

"Wait, you're a slave? How can René stand that? How can you?"

"It is the way it needs to be for right now. I have no worries that when father passes, René will free us. For now, I get to run the household, that is, until you take it over."

Damica laughed at the idea of her running a house, especially one this large.

"If I can help you with anything, I will, but otherwise, I will leave it in your capable hands. Really, this was just the best way for both René and I to meet our needs. I am not sure how much of the lady of the house I will be. I would like to have a garden if possible. And maybe some lessons on what to plant here and when."

"Oh yes! René said you were a leaf doctor like Grand'Mere. We can work together on that if you don't mind, I have a bit of an interest in that as well."

"Oh my goodness! I forgot to tell René, but your Grand' Mere gave me a book, one full of herbs and remedies. You should have it. It is from your family."

"We are your family now too, and if she gave it to you, there was a reason." Angelica smiled at Damica, "I am so glad that she accepted you! Let me leave you to get comfortable. Come on down when you are ready for some cold tea and something to eat."

They enjoyed cold tea and sandwiches out on the big wrap-around porch as the afternoon passed pleasantly. People that worked there came up to meet Damica. They all seemed so happy to see her. A large gathering was planned for the next day with everyone on the plantation so they could all meet and get to know each other.

As dark began to fall, everyone scurried off to their homes. Damica could see the lights in the windows of the small cottages before the mosquitos chased them inside.

As she sat down in the large dining room with René, Two made his first appearance of the day, followed by a white cat with grey tabby spots on her. They jumped up on the table and began to clean each other.

"Favorite, get down. You know better!" scolded René.

"Umm, Favorite. That's what you named the cat?"

"Yes, she's my favorite, obviously."

"Two and Favorite, you are a man that cleverly names his pets," Damica said with a touch of sarcasm in her voice. René laughed so hard he almost shot water out his nose, not something the grown son of one of the wealthiest men on this side of the Atlantic was used to.

The evening passed in companionable contentment. Damica was very glad she had taken René up on his offer, even if he was awful at naming cats.

As she settled down in her new room for the night, she was the happiest she had been since she left her home in France. The doors to the balcony were thrown wide open to catch the cool night air, and the mosquito netting that hung around her big four-poster bed swung lazily in the breeze. The scent of the jasmine and bougainvillea was the last thing she remembered as she drifted off to sleep.

The beating of drums in the distance woke her up. It took her a minute to realize where she was. The cat curled up, snoring next to her, made her feel safe and secure. She lay there on her side, curled up around Two, listening to the rhythm in the distance. She slowly got up to see what it was.

As she stepped out onto the balcony, Two jumped up on the rail and rubbed up against her, purring. She could not see where the noise was coming from. Her room looked out on the marsh, and the drums were coming from the area that housed the inhabitants of the plantation. As she leaned into the railing to listen to the beat mixed with the sounds of the marsh, she realized she could hear a type of chanting.

She could not make out words, just rhythms. Nothing that put her on edge, so she picked up the cat and crawled back into her massive bed, falling back to sleep with the beat reverberating in her head.

Chapter Seventeen

The day started early; the birds were chittering in the marsh, and the people that worked the plantation were up and moving even though Damica was sure they had been up most of the night. She dressed in her lightest frock, promising herself to have a new wardrobe made as soon as she could, and headed down for breakfast. The meal was set up on the veranda that looked out over the pastures where the horses grazed. Damica thought that things could not get any better than this. She was so happy she almost didn't notice when René had come out. He looked stunning in a pair of riding breeches and a light shirt, his boots were shined, and he carried a pair of riding gloves in his hands. He smiled at Damica, who caught herself staring open-mouthed at him.

"I've made arrangements with Angelica to have a seamstress out today so you can get some more appropriate frocks for the weather. Please get whatever you need. We will need some ball gowns as well. I am not sure your black gown will woo anyone other than me." He seemed to smile at the memory of her trying not to get a husband. "I am going to ride the property with a few of the men, make notes of major repairs that need to be done, and maybe make some minor repairs while we are out. It will be a long day, but I will be back in time for our celebration."

"Alright, but you better make it back in time, or it won't be the same. It will be a search party to drag you back!" Damica said with a smile. "Is there anything I can do to help out while you are gone? I really don't care to just be here; I want to be part of here."

"Oh, I fully intend to teach you all about how to run this place. Besides needing the help, I know there is no way to stop you from getting involved. If you know how to work it, you won't get hurt. For the next few days, maybe, just hang out and get comfortable. You need new dresses and some riding clothes. Angelica has already spoken to the cook and some of the men about preparing a space for you to have a garden next to the kitchen garden. I think just those things and learning your way around the property and house should keep you busy for a day or so. And everyone is excited to meet you, so you may need some time to slip away and not be the center of attention." He smiled as he kissed her on the forehead and walked out. Yes, Damica was sure she would like it here.

As Angelica cleared the breakfast, she offered to take Damica into the kitchen to meet Cook.

"You really should meet her. She is the nicest, sweetest lady and will make sure to keep all your favorite foods and to cook them for you, that is if she likes you." Angelica winked at her. Damica tried to help her carry the dishes back into the kitchen, but Angelica swatted her away, "No, this is my job. You will have plenty to do once you get settled."

The cook was an older lady with midnight dark skin and short hair. She kept the kitchen organized in such a way that Damica knew this would be a favorite room in the house. Cook asked her about what she liked to eat and grow. If they were going to be sharing garden space, there would be no need to double plant. She showed her where the sweets were kept and how to open the ice box if she needed anything, then shoed the girls out so she could start working on the meal for the evening. The girls hustled down to the ladies' parlor, where the seamstress was awaiting Damica.

The seamstress was a woman that also worked on the plantation. She was very serious and quiet. Damica stood on a stool as she did the measurements and discussed fabrics and styles. They were in the middle of a deep discussion on which color would look best on her when one of the housemen came in with a letter for Damica.

She stepped down from the stool, full of excitement to see which of the girls from the ship had messaged her. Since they were the only people who knew she was here, she guessed it had to be one of them. Her face paled as she read the note. It was from one of the girls she had been on the ship with. Marie.

Marie inquired about her health, made a little small talk about how the weather was so different here than in France, but then the tone of the letter changed.

Marie mentioned Appolline's disappointment that she had chosen a rich man over everlasting life and power. She then went on to mention that, of course, there was no way that Damica could have taken such a position as that would have upset Jeanne, so she thanked her for not taking Appolline's offer. The letter ended with Marie promising to see her that night. Damica was so taken aback she had to sit down, much to the annoyance of the seamstress. Damica dismissed her and continued to sit and stare out at nothing. This was how Angelica found her when she whooshed back into the room to see how things were going. Not knowing what to do, she handed the note to Angelica, who read it but was confused.

"I don't understand. Who is this."

Damica sighed, "She was my friend on the ship over. Have you heard any of the rumors about our ship?"

"Damica, we might have a good life here, but we are forbidden to leave the plantation. People of our color are rarely treated well or given the time of day for rumors."

"Oh, I'm sorry, I wasn't thinking. Umm, there was an issue with some of the girls that were on the ship, umm, a ummm, disease of sorts."

Damica tried her best to figure out how to tell Angelica about Appolline and the others, but it just seemed too odd to be real.

"One of the sick women took a fancy to me. Apparently, she is very powerful over here and did not need to marry, nor was she asked to. She wanted me to be part of her household." She left it at that, a heavy silence descending on the room.

"As her lover?" Angelica's eyes were the size of saucers.

"I'm not exactly sure. You know that I am a leaf doctor like your Grand'Mere, but I can do a few other things as well. I think she was more interested in the other things than in *other things.*"

Damica was bright red by this time. She tried to look at Angelica in such a way that she would understand. The girl started to giggle, which sent Damica into a fit of giggling. Soon they were laughing so hard that neither could breathe. Big tears were rolling down their faces.

As they settled down, Angelica said, "I'm sorry. I know this is serious, but your face was just so funny. I couldn't help myself." She took a deep breath and wiped her face, "Tell me what we need to do and what it is they want? Did you have plans to see them tonight? How is your friend part of this group?"

Damica sighed. She might as well confide in Angelica since René already knew. "It wasn't quite a disease. They were vampires." Damica's head dropped as if she had something to be ashamed of.

"Oh well, that makes sense then. René had us do a ritual of protection last night. He wasn't sure how far it would work, so we just tried to get the houses covered. We were going to come through tonight to the big house. He did say that as long as no one was invited inside, you should be safe." She smiled encouragingly at the shocked Damica. "You do know he has his own set of powers, right? He is one of the most powerful servants of the spirits in the new world, well, even just on this side of the world."

"I'm not even sure what that means. I know when Appolline confronted us, she called him that."

"Oh, well, it's like magic, ummm, some of the white people call it voodoo, but that has a bad connotation. You will also hear them call René the Shadow Man. They believe that he can manipulate the shadows to do his bidding. The truth is he works hard to get what he wants, and yes, he gets a little help from the other side on occasion but nothing that isn't for the greater good. Like last night. He asked the shadows for help protecting us from the vampires. Nothing in it for him. If he did it for his own gain, it would be bad. Very,very bad. But since he is always working the shadows for the good fortune of others, good fortune abounds for him. That's how it works."

Damica was not really stunned, or not as much as she felt she should be. She had seen René work some magic the other night, and they had blended that magic.

She stopped and thought for a moment. Maybe that was why he was so comfortable with her because he thought she could work the magic too. She smiled a bit to herself. Maybe she could if she had the right teacher. Her family had only ever worked with leaves and nature, but maybe there was a whole other area of magic and witchcraft that she hadn't even thought she could explore.

"I am happy to hear he works for others; I hope I can learn some from him and all of you." She hugged Angelica tight, so happy to be somewhere that she was accepted.

Chapter Eighteen

The celebration was a huge success. Cook outdid herself, making all of Damica's favorites as well as many of the local dishes. The workers came and danced and sang. Everyone introduced themselves to Damica, who got up and danced with anyone that asked. She sang silly songs with the children and laughed and giggled with the women. She felt right at home.

As the families went home with sleeping children or tired adults, she tried to help Cook and Angelica clean up, both of whom tried their best to shoo her away. René laughed at the interaction but just sat back and watched his new wife bully and cajole her way into helping clean up after the party until she came over and dragged him up to help carry things in. Both Cook and Angelica were stunned that he did it with a smile on his face. They smiled knowingly at each other as they watched the couple go into the house.

"Thank you, sir, for helping us," smirked Damica.

"Anytime, my dear," René could not help but laugh. He found he laughed a lot around her, even if their marriage was one of convenience. He was happy she had agreed to come live here. He was also happy to see how well she fit into his world and how much all the important people in his life genuinely liked her.

"Angelica told me about the ritual you did last night. I think we need to have a word." The smile melted off René's face as he saw how serious Damica was.

"Okay, how about we head to the library. There are a few things I would like to show you as well."

The two walked side by side to the library, which was just fine with Damica since she wasn't even sure where the library was.

"I'm sorry if the ritual offended you. It is just what we do here. I should have asked Angelica to not say anything."

Damica was momentarily taken aback before she realized how serious her statement about it had been.

"No, no, René, that was not what I needed to talk to you about. Well, it kind of is, but not in the way that you think. I do not mind any of that. In fact, I would like to learn a bit of it."

She stood awkwardly staring at the books around her, sighed, then reached in the pocket of her dress, took the letter she had received earlier out of her pocket, and handed it to him without a word. As he read it, his countenance darkened.

He looked at her, "I haven't protected the house yet. I was hoping to have a few days."

She just looked at him. He was getting angrier the longer he stood there.

"I will sleep in your parlor tonight. We will send Angelica and Cook home now, we can finish cleaning, or it can wait until morning."

He strode out of the room to send the women on their way. He made sure they each had a torch to light the way, no lanterns tonight. Fire was their friend. As she watched her friends head home, out of the dark came two small figures so low to the ground. Damica only noticed the movement, not the shape. Her heart began to race as they moved closer and closer to her. They seemed too small to be human of any kind, but she had heard tales of shapeshifting vampires. She was about to turn and run when she heard a familiar eerp.

"Two! You scared me!" she scooped one of the cats up in her arms and hugged him tight. He didn't seem to mind and began to purr. Favorite weaved her way between Damicas legs until she stopped cuddling Two long enough to reach down and pet the pretty little cat. "You two should be ashamed of yourselves, scaring me like that. I have it in my mind not to let you sleep with me!" At which Two made himself quite comfortable up on her shoulder.

"I'm not sure you have a choice in the matter. He did follow you all the way from Hispaniola to be with you. I think he has chosen where and when he will be with you, whether you like it or not. Are you ready to head up?"

Damica was a bit nervous but nodded her head. Part of her was afraid that René would try something before she was ready. Part of her was hoping he would.

"Yes," was all she managed to squeak out before they headed up. Two still on her shoulder and Favorite running up beside René. If anyone was in the house to see them, they would have made quite the sight.

René kept his word and settled into Damicas sitting room. They left the door slightly ajar between the two rooms. Neither one wanted to leave the big French doors open even though it was the only source of cool air to be had.

Damica lay in the big dark room, which she had loved the night before. Tonight she was sweating and feeling miserable about the situation. She was sad that she had brought this danger to this lovely home. She felt safe here, but was she really? Would she be safe anywhere? She could hear René murmuring to the cat. At least, she hoped it was the cat.

"Are you talking to the cat?"

"Maybe, would it make me crazy if I was?" Damica smiled at that.

"No, it would make you crazy if you were just in there talking to nothing."

"Then it was definitely the cat."

The night settled around them, and Damica drifted off to sleep with a smile on her face.

Chapter Nineteen

Hissing and growling startled Damica awake. A slight breeze wafted through the room as she watched the cat grow in agitation at whatever was bothering him. It took Damica longer than it should have to get her senses enough to sit up and look around. Her French doors were flung open, there stood a silhouette of a person on her balcony. She yelled for René, whose cursing could be heard as he tried to get past his cat, who was doing her best to trip him up and keep him safe.

"Damica, Damica, it's me. Marie. May I come in? I have missed you so much! I miss playing quadrille with you and telling stories. Please let me in."

The voice seemed so pathetic and whiney, nothing like the energetic girl that Damica had known. She quietly began to weep for her lost friend.

"Don't fall for it. She is not who you knew," whispered René from the darkened room. He had made his way into her room and was doing something on the floor by the foot of her bed.

"I know: she cannot fool me. I just miss my friend. This is not her anymore."

The wail that came from outside was so mournful it could have broken Damicas heart had she not known what tricksters' vampires could be.

"Damica, how could you forget me! How could you leave me like this! Please let me come in so we can talk, laugh, and be as close as we were on the ship!"

Damica grabbed Two and buried her face in the cat, who continued to puff up his hair at the vampire while Maire continued to plead to come in.

She glanced to the side when she heard chanting or singing. She wasn't quite sure which. René had set up some candles on the floor and was singing in a powerful yet pleading way, asking for protection and help but using names she had never heard before. It reminded her of the hymns she would hear from the churches back home, but not quite. It was the same but different somehow, not just the names but the tone.

A screech from the balcony drew her attention back as Marie attempted to come inside. A sharp ping followed by a spark lit up the night as the vampire was thrown off the balcony.

Damica started to run out to check on her, but René grabbed her arm.

"Don't. It may break the protection. I've asked the Loa for protection, but since she was already here, I'm not sure how much we will be given. Do you have any plants we can hang at the doors? "

Both René and Damica jumped back, Damica falling backward across the bed with a very annoyed cat flying from her arms as two bodies slammed into the balcony.

"Hello, Damica, nice place you got yourself," purred Jeanne. She had Marie by the hair.

The younger vampire was squirming and whimpering to get away, but Jeanne held on fast.

"It seems as if one more person wants you. Everyone wants you," she continued to speak softly, menacingly, "What is it that you have that I don't? Huh? I am powerful, beautiful, rich, all the things I was when she turned me. We had it all, Appolline and I, until you came along. And this one, this one cries for you, like you were her savior or something. You couldn't save her! You failed!"

She screamed those last two words at Damica as she pulled Marie's head back and sliced her throat so deep that only a few tendons held her head on her body. Marie's eyes held a look of shock. Jeanne ripped the rest of the skin and tendons as she pulled off the head and threw it at the open door. It bounced off the protective magic and rolled back to the body that had begun to slowly slump to the ground.

Jeanne let out an animalistic scream, "Even now, you mock me! You can't stay protected forever! Vengeance will be mine!" She hopped up on the banister and jumped, disappearing into the night.

Damica and René stood horrified at the sight of Marie's body. Slowly they looked at each other.

René came to Damica, "My love, you are shaking. Let's go into the sitting room, away from this mess."

For all his brave words, he was paler than Damica had ever seen him. His eyes were the size of saucers.

"We can rest on the settee, or we can go find other rooms for the night, Damica. Come with me."

He gently prodded her to move in the direction of the sitting room; Two was already in there with Favorite. They were both looking out at their people with wide eyes as if to say, *hurry up, let's shut the door and be done with this.*

They managed to get to the settee in the other room before Damica collapsed into René's arms, shaking and crying.

"That was horrible! She did not deserve that end. She just wanted to come here and find love and be happy. I should have saved her; I should have known what they were doing to her. I should have saved her! I shouldn't have come here. Look at all the danger I brought. How can you be so calm when I might very well have brought destruction down upon your home."

René wrapped his arms around her, "Shhh, it will be okay, shhhh." He began to rock her gently, "There was no help for her. Once she was bit, there was nothing you could have done to save her. She was going to die as a vampire or by your hand on the ship. You didn't know. You did your best for all of them. In the end, I think she knew that, and I think she wanted you to know that as well. As for everyone here, they know what's going on. Didn't you see the lights of the houses lit? They are aware that the battle has begun. Let's try to sleep and worry about the rest tomorrow, okay?"

Damica tried to stay awake, but the emotional toll from the last few minutes, was it really just minutes? Plus, all the excitement from the last few days was catching up with her. Her eyes closed, and the last thing she remembered was feeling René's arms around her.

Chapter Twenty

With the weight of the cat on her chest, and the bright sun streaming through the window, Damica was forced to wake. Her neck hurt, her back hurt, and she felt as though she had spent too much time enjoying the night. As she swung her legs over the settee, the events of the hours before came crashing back on her, and she most definitely did not spend it in enjoyment. Her first thought was to rush over and check on Marie's body. Her own body was not entirely up to the task of rushing. Sleeping on the settee had done a number on her. She tried to stretch a bit as she moved through the door, Two at her side, yowling to be fed. As she entered the room and peeked out onto the balcony, she saw a small pile of ash.

"I guess they really do burn to ash in the sun."

She turned as René walked into the room. He handed her a cup of chicory and smiled. "I thought you might need a pick me up this morning."

Damica smiled and kissed him on the cheek in thanks.

"I've talked to Cook and Angelica. They said they could see some of last night. Mostly what they saw was a green haze over the house; that would have been the protection I asked for. I think today, we need to work together to keep ourselves and our people safe. I can teach you some of what I do and would love to learn a little of what you do."

"I think that is a good plan." Damica smiled up at him, "Is there any business that needs to be taken care of today or for the week? We might want to get whatever needs done, done."

"We are pretty self-sufficient here. No need to go to town. Most of the business has been taken care of. It's time to get safe and in order. Once this is taken care of, I will gladly teach you how to run the plantation. Then I can take some time off."

René smiled a wicked smile at Damica, and she laughed. The coffee was stronger than what she was used to, and she was feeling jittery already. She shooed him out of the room so she could change and they could get the preparation started. As she turned toward the still-open French doors, an envelope fluttered through and landed on the floor.

With a big sigh, Damica started toward the letter just as Two pounced on it.

"Give that to me, you rascal," she chuckled at the silliness of the cat, happy for the distraction. Sighing again, she took the envelope from the cat.

"What now, really I just want some time that's normal, or at least time to find out what normal is going to be here."

My Dearest Damica,

I wanted to make you aware that both Jeanne and Marie have not been seen at the house for over a day. I hope this note finds you safe. Jeanne is not a fan of yours and has said on numerous occasions that she wishes you dead.

Your loving servant

Appolline

Thanks for the heads up, thought Damica. She was sure that Appolline knew that Jeanne had been missing for a while. She was also confident that Appolline thought she could somehow use this to her advantage to get Damica to go to her. Damica was hoping that that would never happen. She was hopeful that between her and René, they would be strong enough to protect what was theirs.

Breakfast was served in the kitchen with Cook and Angelica. The four of them started making plans to protect the plantation and its people. Damica showed them all the letter and explained that it had just flown into her room as if the wind had brought it. René sat quiet while the ladies discussed where to find the plants that Damica would need.

"It's disturbing that the letter just flew in. It makes me think she may be more powerful than we originally anticipated. We should be grateful that it was the other one that showed up last night and not

Appolline. Can you tell us anything you know about her? Did she show any power on the ship?"

Damica thought about it for a few moments, took a deep breath then told them about the voyage. About the deal she had made with Appolline to keep everyone safe. How her plants and minor enchantments had kept them all safe and well, even when she was sitting face to face with the vampire. By the end of the story, the three listeners were staring wide-eyed at her, their mouths agape.

"You've worked with plants your whole life, it's probably why the sleeping plants did not work on you, or it could be your own magic. I think you are more powerful than you know." René stood and walked over to her, "That was very brave of you to sacrifice yourself to keep the others safe."

"I'm not sure if I have magic. The plants, I can understand. My family has always worked with nature to make things better. My mother taught me how to protect myself, no magic, just intention, I guess would be the word."

René chuckled, "Intention is the most important part of magic, my love. I think between us, we have a very good chance of keeping everything safe, especially you. You have caught the attention of an incredibly powerful creature. I think she can feel the magic you have and wants to possess it."

Damica blushed, "I didn't tell you everything. Umm, she, well, she," Damica sighed, "She wanted us to live together as lovers."

One of the men from the stables walked in just at that moment. He cleared his throat, which made Damica blush even more. "Madame, these flowers were left with your name on them right outside the stables. I thought I should bring them to you."

Damica reached out and took the roses the groom held, "Thank you for bringing them in." She forced a smile as they dismissed the man. "Roses, I used dried roses to keep the vampires out." She let the roses slip from her hand.

"Well then, we will use this to keep this vampire away." Angelica scooped up the flowers and began to sort them to dry. "Now, you two get going. There is a lot to do. A vampire is scary enough, but if this one is as powerful as you say, well, then we are going to need all the help we can get."

René and Damica spent the morning roaming the property looking for plants that could be used to protect them all from the vampires. Damica used her own knowledge as well as Grand'Mere's book.

A few of the plants they came across from the book that Damica had not used before were night-blooming Jessamine and morning glories. Where she would have used Wolfsbane in France, this was not a plant found in the humid environment she now lived in. Many of the plants in Grand'Mere's book were not only used to keep vampires away but could be highly poisonous to people as well.

As they walked, Damica taught René what they were looking for and what it could be used for. How each plant they collected could help in specific ways. She also pointed out plants that she could use for other things, but today was not the day to collect those.

René was a good student, asking questions and paying attention to all the subtleties each plant could produce. By the time they were headed back to the house, he had a good grasp of what it was that Damica did, as well as how it was done.

He was impressed with her knowledge and skill when it came to using nature to protect and care for people.

"I believe we should see what type of wood would be best for stakes, though I would prefer to keep them farther away than that. I really don't want to have to get up close and personal with them." René contemplated, "I think some of these will work. It's called Green Ashe; it's as close to Rowan as we grow here. Should we go to the kitchen garden? I do know that garlic is one way to stop them, and I know there is a lot of garlic growing right now."

Damica agreed, and they began to walk back toward the house. A small child ran through the woods toward them, laughing and enjoying the day. He ran up to René and pretended to sword fight with the man, who was more than happy to play with the child.

Damica watched this interaction with a smile. René pretended that the child had made a mortal wound on him and proceeded to dramatically die, making the child laugh and whoop his delight before he ran off back toward his home.

Laughing, Damica reached out to help René up, "That was an excellent death. I'm sure that young man is very proud of it."

"I do what I can to help."

He took her hand and stood, stumbling a bit as he got up so that her face was pressed into his chest. Laughing, his arms reached around her. Without thinking, she rested her forehead on him, thinking how nice he smelled, like cinnamon and wood smoke. She looked up at him and smiled.

"I forget how small you are. You are so capable and strong, stubborn and hardheaded; sometimes, you seem larger than me." He laughed as he said this, though Damica wasn't sure how to take that and frowned at him. "It's a compliment, I promise!" He leaned down to kiss her just as the young boy ran back out of the woods, but there was no joy on his face this time, just fear.

"Monsieur René, Monsieur René, you are needed in the field. Hurry, hurry!" He grabbed René by the hand and tried to run with him.

René looked back at Damica and then took off running with the boy. Damica lifted her skirts and jogged after them, holding onto her bag of herbs and plants. She soon realized she couldn't keep up or hold on to everything and run without almost tripping. She slowed her pace, straightened her skirt and hair, and walked quickly in the direction they had headed.

As she got closer, she could hear yelling. Along with the yelling, she could hear René calling for calm. She emerged from the trees into the field, momentarily blinded by the sun. When she could finally see, there seemed to be dark mounds all over the pasture. It took her brain a moment to realize that the mounds were cattle. About twenty of them, she could hear the flies and smell the sweet scent of rot.

Covering her nose so she could breathe, she stepped up next to René. He stood with his fists on his hips, staring over the destruction. His face was drawn, his lips tight. Quietly he said, "They did this. They will try to hurt us in any way. We need to think bigger, Damica. We need to protect our animals and people. How are we going to do that?" He rubbed his face and sighed.

"Can we collect the rest of the herd and keep them closer to the house?"

"Yes, we can," he answered quietly. "But how do we protect the crops."

"I don't know, but we will figure it out. Let's get the herd moved and get the hogs and chickens up close too. Bury or burn these." She hugged him and turned to the crowd to give directions.

René reached out and took her hand as she was giving instructions on moving the animals. He gave her hand one last squeeze, then gathered some of the younger, stronger men and began to organize a bonfire for the carcasses.

They worked together to keep their people calm and get things done. The days were longer here, but evening was getting near. They would need to hurry if they were going to keep everyone safe for the night.

Damica pulled up as much garlic as she could find and distributed it to the homes while the men and children gathered the animals in close. The burning would go on through the evening, so it was up to Damica to get the houses and the people here in order.

She looked through Grand'Mere's book to see what she could do to keep the animals safe. There were what seemed to be spells in the back of the book.

Intention is the most important part of any of this. If you are missing an element, just use your intention.

"Intention, okay, Damica, you can do this." She said to herself quietly. "You can keep them all safe, or you are just a crazy person. I think tonight you might find the answer to that."

She stood on the edge of where the cattle and hogs were contained. She cleared her mind and thought of the shield she put around herself. Then she thought of it as part of her, a part she could leave behind to form a wall, and began to walk around the corrals. She wasn't sure if it was working, but she was sweating with effort. When she finished the walk, she looked up.

"Let it be closed," and she could see the light around the corrals. She also noticed that the sun was setting, darkness was creeping in.

"That looks amazing, Damica! I thought you said you didn't know magic?" René walked to her, smelling of smoke and burnt meat. He had soot on his cheek. It took everything in her to not wipe it away.

"I wasn't sure I could. I just thought of the shield my mother taught me and used what your Grand'Mere wrote in her book. I hope it's enough."

He hugged her close, "I think it will be fine." He looked up at the sky as he let her go, "I don't think we will have time to get to the house and secure it, and I really want to make sure everyone here is safe. Do you mind sleeping here in a cabin? It's not fancy, but I think it will be safe."

Damica agreed to stay. She was too exhausted from the shield to argue, and, honestly, it seemed like the best solution. She headed off to help Cook with a meal for everyone. Cook was using her own cabin to prepare the food for the night.

René started off to gather everyone to help with a ritual to add more protection to the cabins.

Chapter Twenty-One

The cats showed back up just as dinner was being served, it was full dark by this point, and there was a large bonfire in the middle of where the cabins were. Everyone took a plate and ate in silence; the air was thick with anticipation. The cats circled the fire, then proceeded to sit right on the edge of where the protection started.

"How do they know where to sit?" asked Damica.

"They can sense it. Pretty sure Two would be called your familiar in another time and place. He is quite aware of where your magic is.

If he were here when you put it up, it would not have taken as much out of you, and it could very well have made it more powerful. Favorite does that for me at times, though my magic is a different flavor, so a lot depends solely on me and my intention.

"Intention is one of those things that flows through all flavors of magic. Are you ready to help me with the ritual?" He said as he stood up and brushed dirt off his trousers. "I know you don't think you can help, but really, you can help lend your power if you're feeling up to it."

Damica smiled and nodded. She was exhausted emotionally and physically, but he had been such a good student for her that she felt as though she owed it to him to be a good student for him. And to be honest, they did not have a lot of time to learn. They weren't sure what the night would bring.

"One of the most essential elements within my flavor of magic are the four cardinal directions. When I am singing, I am calling on them to help or hurt, as the case may be. In most of my workings, I am asking for help for others. I call on the help of Lao, or the gods, to help me as well. I sing to them my request, though it might sound more like a chant.

"I offer them tributes or gifts. They like Rum, fresh fruit, coins, or interesting beads. It's my magic, but I am asking them to direct it and to help enhance it. I am on good terms with them. They usually try to help, but I need to make sure to keep them happy. If they turn on me or think that I have not honored them enough, they can take my soul. Or wreak havoc on my life.

"Never do harm when good can solve the problem.

"Intention, like with your magic, is the most important part.

If your intention is good, you are safe.

Keep that in your heart, Damica. Keep your intention good."

René stepped up to the fire, put his arms in the air, raised his face to the light and heat of the flame, and began to chant. He walked around the flame as he marked the four cardinal directions and called to the Lao for protection. René continued to chant while he tossed a plate full of food into the fire as a gift to the Lao. He then took Damicas hand and whispered "intention" into her ear.

She wasn't sure if he meant to try to do magic like him or do her own. She swayed along with the rhythm of the chant but decided to do what she was familiar with.

She closed her eyes and thought about a protective wall she had placed earlier in the day around the cabins, the people, and the animals. She saw the wall get thicker and stronger, turning a light purple as René's intention was mixed with hers. She felt satisfied that they were all safe.

Until she heard a slow clap coming from what seemed only a few yards away. She opened her eyes just as Two let out an awful howl.

Appolline was standing just on the other side of the shield, clapping. Favorite stood next to René, all puffed up, facing the opposite direction than Appolline was.

Damica turned to see Jeanne at the other end of the cabins just outside the shield. She sighed in relief, realizing that the vampires could not enter, or they would have already.

Almost in unison, the cats climbed on their shoulders, Two on Damica and Favorite on René. As the cat settled on her, Damica could feel her energy become more, like she had gotten stronger just from the little cat being with her. She stood up taller. All the exhaustion from the day left her. Her vision seemed to be clearer, and she could feel her heartbeat. The strong, steady beat focused her mind.

"I see you have found your place, Damica, here in the cabins of the underlings. It's funny, I can give you so much more, yet here you are. With him. And them."

She waved her hands, encompassing everyone and everything; a sneer crossed her face. She put her hand out in a come here gesture, "All you need to do is come with me, Damica."

There was power behind her words, but Damica could resist it with ease, especially with the cat on her.

"NO!" the word resonated from all around her as René stood tall in front of her.

"She has made her choice, and you were not it, vampire. Leave here and never come back!"

Appolline's laughter echoed around them, bouncing off the walls of the cabins.

"Shadow man, you might be able to banish me for the night but think twice before you banish me for good. Remember, I am not the most dangerous vampire here."

At that moment, Jeanne began attacking the shield like a wild animal, screaming at the top of her lungs. Damica wondered how she had not heard it before.

"I could just leave her here to kill you all. Eventually, she would get through the shield. She has gone thoroughly insane at this point. Jealousy is a dangerous thing."

At that, the wind began to pick up, it felt as if a storm was about to roll in, yet the sky was clear, "I will take her with me tonight, but tomorrow I may not be as generous."

The wind picked up Jeanne as she screamed, Appolline lifted gracefully into the air. They both flew away on the wind. One smiling benevolently, one screaming manically.

"How did you do that?" whispered Damica so only René could hear her.

"It's what I am. I am shadows. My power is strongest in the light within the darkness and dawn itself when the world is ruled by shadows. Your power comes from the light and sun, in the growth of the herbs and flowers you use. The combination makes us more powerful than they are, at least I hope it does."

I pray you are right, thought Damica as she wrapped her arms around him to feel his warmth. She shivered, not from cold but from something else.

Chapter Twenty-Two

The light filtered in through the window, waking Damica. It took her a moment to realize where she was. She and René had spent the night in the cottage of Cook, who was humming and making cafe au lait for the morning.

"Morning Madame, I have some coffee for you. I'm sorry, I don't have much food here. Coffee and toast will have to start the day until we head back to the main house. I will make sure to have a large mid-day meal."

The older woman smiled as she handed Damica a cup filled with coffee and lovely foamed milk. Damica closed her eyes and took in the warm scent, which made her feel safe and cozy, happy that this place was now her home.

"Cook, might I ask you a question?"

"Yes, Madame, anything," Cook said as she nodded.

"What is your name? We all just call you Cook, but what is your name?"

The older woman chuckled, "Mary, my name is Mary. But no one has called me that since my husband died." Her face grew sad, but she quickly shook it off. "It's okay that I am called Cook. It doesn't bother me."

"If it's alright with you, I would like to call you Mary. We are going through so much together. I feel as though I owe you the respect."

The idea that anyone owed her respect made Mary stop and stare at Damica, then she walked over and hugged the younger woman.

"Thank you, Madame. I appreciate that. I am so happy you are here to help us stay safe; René is so powerful, but with you, it is so much more. And you make him smile. I have not seen that boy smile since he was a child. Thank you for giving that back to us."

René stepped into the house at that moment and took in the scene.

"Mary and I were just discussing the beauty of this coffee she made. It is the best thing I have tasted in my life!"

Damica winked at Mary, who smiled and went back to her stove.

" Come, help me gather our things, darling. I think we may need to get the house secure tonight. My back may not be kind to me if we keep sleeping on the floor."

The day had dawned hot and humid, the men were in the field, and the women that worked in the house were waiting for them to lead the way.

Everywhere they looked, there was wind damage to the trees and buildings outside of their protective bubble. When they reached the house, the doors and windows were blown open. Anything close to the door or light in weight was blown around, but nothing was destroyed.

The cats pranced from room to room almost as if they were showing everyone all the damage while pointing out how much worse it could have been.

"It seems they cannot enter even when we are not here, but I am glad we all stayed together last night. I think you are right; we need to get the house protected."

They set about putting all the rooms back together. Mary started her promised mid-day meal while Damica set up all the herbs and plants she had collected the day before on the dining room table. She needed to prepare to dry the ones that would be better that way and pull out the ones she could use that evening.

Angelica burst into the room just as the last of the plants to be dried were wrapped for hanging.

"There is a strange man here. He is demanding to see you. Damica, he looks all beat up and crazy! The groom was up talking with me, so he stayed behind to keep the man out while I came to fetch you."

"I'll go, but please go get René. I think he is upstairs preparing for tonight."

There was a loud crash from the front of the house, Damica sighed, annoyed that she could not find a normal day, and hurried to see who it was.

Charles was standing over the young man who had been unlucky enough to be speaking with Angelica when he had arrived.

"Charles, you were not invited into my home. How dare you hurt my people!" She helped the young man up, making sure he was okay. The only thing that seemed to be hurt was his pride. She turned on the older man, "How dare you! Leave now! I do not wish to see you again, do not step foot on my property again!"

Charles fell to his knees before Damica, "Mercy, I claim mercy! Please, mademoiselle, keep me safe from those monsters! When they returned this morning, they beat me and tried to kill me. Look at the state I am in, mercy please show mercy!" He stood with his arms and hands out as if to show her all the damage he had taken the night before.

There were a number of bruises and cuts, but Damica was not about to buy the act. She didn't know why, but it did not feel right.

"If that's the truth, why are you not dead?" René asked as he stepped up to Damica. Charles threw himself back on the floor in a groveling manner, looking up at them to plead his case with his eyes.

"I promise on God's name that they tried to kill me. I need help and have nowhere else to go!"

René put his hand out as if he was feeling the air. Damica could feel it, too, though she wasn't sure what it was. With a snap of his hand, René pulled the magic off of Charles to reveal that he was fine, with no bruises, his clothes were perfect and neat. Charles's face contorted with rage.

"We could have ended this so easily. You let me in, I invite them in, no one dies but you," he spat at René, "Appolline would have her, and we could all go." He lunged at the younger man, who easily put the man back down.

"I suppose I can't have you going back to tell them. What shall we do with you? Shall we kill you? I am not usually into human sacrifice, but I may make an exception!" René spat.

Now that the magic was gone from the air, Damica could taste René's rage on the tip of her tongue. His fists were clenched at his sides, his mouth was pursed in anger, and she could visibly see him shaking just slightly from the intense emotion.

"Please don't, René. Isn't there some horrible place we can put him until this is over?"

A sneer came across René's handsome face, making her glad she had never made him angry. For all that she did not want to get married, she was happy here. She was growing fond of René and could not wait for the day they could just be together without any of the anger or drama that had surrounded them from the beginning. She would have to remember that for all his gentleness and love he showed her, he was not a man to cross.

"I have the perfect place for him, the hole. It's a literal hole my father used to use to punish his....people....before he gave this place to me. It fills with water and muck, snakes, and twigs. Or sometimes it is high and dry and just full of spiders and snakes. I think that will be a good spot, it might kill him to go in there, but I will not be doing the killing. Is that acceptable to you, my love?"

Damica nodded quietly, knowing it was the best solution. She was not happy with the idea of leaving a man in the swamp. René picked up Charles and dragged him out into the trees.

Damica quietly walked up the stairs to her rooms, tears rolling down her face. She sat on her bed, looking out on the balcony where her friend Marie had died, focusing past that spot to the beautiful countryside of her new home, wondering what she should do to keep everyone safe.

"You better not be thinking of leaving. You know we would all hunt you down." Angelica walked in without knocking, carrying a tray of tea and cookies. "We know these woods and swamps better than you ever will, well maybe, and we would drag you back. You have brought excitement and love back to this place. You have brought hope back to our home, and when you are me, that's more important than anything. I don't have control over anything, neither does René, honestly, even though father has given him his freedom, he still has to do what he's told.

"You, you have crossed the ocean to start a life. You traveled with vampires and stayed alive. You kept most of those with you alive. You walked off the ship knowing you were different, a witch, and kept your head held high. You did not compromise, well maybe a little by marrying my brother, but you are hope that maybe someday we can all make our own way like you have.

"Now have some tea and cookies that Cook made, dust yourself off, and come help us prepare for the night. I gave you forty minutes to feel sorry for yourself. Now it's time to get stuff done."

Damica stared up at the young woman who stood with her hands on her hips, her feet slightly apart, scowling down at her.

"Go on, get up. We have things to do. You don't want to spend another night on the floor of Cooks cabin again, do you? Hmmm? I didn't think so. And you know it would be better if you and René actually slept in the same room.

"Of course, I wouldn't want to sleep in his room either. He's a man, so it's messy and smells like hunting and dirty boots. Let's go, let's go." She clapped her hands at Damica to get her moving. Damica stood up with fresh tears in her eyes and gave the young woman a hug.

She wiped the tears from her face, "Thank you, thank you for accepting me into your family even though you don't really know me. Thank you because I brought all this trouble to you all."

"Damica, this trouble was coming one way or another. These monsters are here. Some have been here for God only knows how long. People have disappeared. Not many and not all that often, but we don't matter. I don't matter. To René, we do, but to the rest of society, we don't matter.

"We are prey, easy prey. We have had three people in the last three years disappear, other plantations have had people disappear as well. You are keeping us all safe. That matters. Thank you!"

Damica was stunned by this revelation. She had no idea the horror these people must have felt, knowing something was taking their kin and not having anywhere to turn. She began to understand why the workers and family on the plantation were so accepting of the rituals that René performed. He was the only person trying to help them. Even before she came to live here, he had been trying to help his people stay alive.

The girls exchanged another hug, then went down to prepare for what the night would bring.

Chapter Twenty-Three

Dark descended upon the plantation. The animals were safe in their protected corral, and the workers were safe within their homes. Damica and René spent the afternoon getting the main house ready. No one asked of Charles or where he was. No one spoke of those missing. Their focus was on the night.

Mary, the cook, and Angelica decided to stay the night in the big house. They had rooms on the same floor as Damica and René, though he was going to sleep in Damicas rooms for the night. They were as prepared as they could be. The house was protected, and each room that was occupied was protected.

The clock chimed every hour. The night became darker and darker; lightning could be seen on the horizon. Mary made sure cafe au lait kept warm in the kitchen with some fresh bread for snacks. Still, the time passed. By early morning, when the sky was still black, but the air was lightening up, René and Damica were exhausted. They had stayed up all day and night. They were pacing the room and playing card games, telling each other stories of their childhood, and just getting to know each other better. Damica lay down on the bed, leaving the door to the balcony open to allow the cooler breeze inside to alleviate the hot night air.

"Well, I guess I should retire to the other room; it has been a lovely evening. Who knew that a lady such as yourself would know so many crass card games and so many unlady-like words when she lost?"

Damica laughed at René's fake outrage.

"My mother and aunts had no trouble teaching me both. Why don't you lay down here with me? It's almost light out, and there should be no need for you to sleep on another floor or couch in your own house."

Damica nervously looked out at him, hoping he would not decide he wanted nothing to do with lying next to her. René paused for a moment before he approached the bed. He sat on the side of it and removed his boots, then laid down next to Damica. They laid on their backs, feeling awkward, hands crossed on both their stomachs until René started to giggle.

"You know, this was not how I pictured the first night I spent in bed with my new bride."

"Same, but not bride, husband...you know what I mean," Damica replied, flustered. ené, still chuckling, rolled over on his side to face her and propped his head up in his hand.

"I love being with you, whether we sleep in the same bed or not. I love spending time with you. I am learning so much about other magics, and I don't have to hide what I am. You're not afraid of me. You can stand up to whatever life throws at you. I love that."

His smile made her stomach do flips. She moved closer to him, snuggling into his warm body. He leaned down and kissed her gently on the lips. She wrapped her arms around him, his scent engulfing her. They both froze in place as the first scream of the night could be heard echoing through the swamps.

Still unmoving, unsure of what they had heard, they tried to convince themselves it was just their imagination or an animal meeting its end. Since they both stopped at the same time, they both knew the sound was real and much too human to be a swamp cat.

René sighed and rolled off the bed to put his boots on. Damica padded barefoot to the balcony, straining to look over in the direction of the cabins, she could see some light in windows, but nothing was moving. The scream echoed again.

"It could be a swamp cat," René said, "they sound eerily human when they call to each other, or it could be something else."

The wind started to pick up even though the sky was clear. They could see the trees moving deep in the swamp. Then silence. No crickets or frogs, no birds or animal noises. It was as if the night had just stopped.

It must have been close to four or five in the morning at this point. The morning songs should have been starting.

A shadow ran out of the woods toward the big house. It was a child's shadow. The same child René had played with in the woods was running for all he was worth toward the house as Appolline and Jeanne descended upon him.

Jeanne tackled him with glee, sending them both tumbling to the ground. The door to the room was ripped open as René took off toward the melee. Damica turned and followed him out, slowed a bit by shock and her skirts, always in the way as she ran.

The scene unfolding in front of her as she ran through the yard was terrifying. The vampire had the child in her arms, René was setting into motion a chant and spell, Appolline stood to the side laughing maniacally at him. The crying of the child was all Damica heard until the cats launched at Jeanne. Then all hell broke loose.

René said some words she didn't understand and threw his hands out in front of him. A ball of blue light struck Jeanne in the center of the chest just as Favorite landed on her head. Appolline started to screech as Two landed on her neck, scratching, clawing, and biting until the vampire got a hold of him and threw him into the trees. The child stood in shock until Damica hollered, "Run!" then he took off back toward the cabins, where a group of people were out in the courtyard yelling for him to hurry.

Damica saw the boy launch himself into a woman's arms before they all ran back into their cabins. She turned in time to see Jeanne and Appolline both jump on René, cats hanging off both women. As the cats and René came in contact with each other, the air burned blue. Damica could hear the sizzle of the vampires as they tried to grab René.

An anger she had never felt before came over her. The shield she had always used to protect herself came up around her and then blew apart into sharp pieces. What looked like purple shards of glass went spinning through the air, pushing the vampires out and off of René.

Cutting them where the jagged pieces had touched. René fell to the ground gasping. Favorite let out a howl as she tried to curl up with him.

Two ran up Damicas dress to sit on her shoulder. She could feel the way his presence bolstered her power. She marched forward to stand in front of René, "Be gone from here!" she bellowed at the vampires, the power in her voice creating a wind that blew them back. "This is not your place!" As she looked up, she noticed dawn was breaking. The vampires noticed as well, and a strong wind picked them both up and shot them into the air. They vanished before the light hit the spot they had been standing.

Damica turned to see blood pooling around René. She ran over to him chanting "No, no, no, no, no," as she went. When she got close, there was no barrier around him, no glowing color engulfing him. In his haste to rescue the child, he had forgotten his shield!

Favorite was curled up on him in such a way that Damica could see that he was still breathing. As she laid a gentle hand on him to turn him towards her, she could see that the vampires had torn his neck apart. He was bleeding to death.

He opened his eyes as she placed his head in her lap, her tears splattered on his face as he smiled up at her and croaked through his ragged neck, "Darkness and dawn, as the shadows lay across the ground, so shall I."

He closed his eyes to get a breath, "Don't cry, my love, power of the dawn, power of the shadow. You will never lose me." He smiled as his eyes closed, and his body went limp. Favorite let out a grief-stricken yowl, soon joined in by Two. The sun peeked over the horizon, creating the shadows of Damica and René stretching long in front of them. René's shadow was not quite matching his solid form, but no one seemed to notice as his workers and family began to pour from the cabins.

Damica held him close, weeping.

Chapter Twenty-Four

It took coercing from Mary and Angelica to get her to leave René. From that moment on, the day was a blur. Angelica somehow got Damica up to her rooms. The scent of René was still on the pillow and sheets. She lay there with her face planted firmly on top of the pillow, breathing in his woodsy scent as her tears dampened the cloth.

Damica wasn't sure what time it was or when people came in to see her. Favorite was carried in, limp, and laid by her side. Two snuggle both of them. At one point, one of the men came in to tell her that body pieces had been found in the swamp. She nodded, too numb to even feel anything.

They assumed it was Charles by the coat that was found nearby. Though they searched for the rest of him to give him a proper burial, his head was never found.

The boy that René saved had been scared by the screaming and had tried to get to the big house where he had been taught to go when bad things happened. It was safe. At some point, the boy's mother came in and cried with Damica, but honestly, she had no recollection of who was in and out and was only later told she had been a comfort to the woman. Angelica came in with some broth and tea from Mary.

René's workers and family began to organize a burial for him. They started by preparing the body as best they could and laid it out in the parlor downstairs. They filled the room with white candles and dressed the body in white. They brought in magnolias and jasmine, the scent of which wafted throughout the house, eventually making its way up to where Damica lay.

As evening approached, Angelica came in and got Damica up. She helped her get cleaned and dressed in a light cotton white dress before she came down for René's celebration. Everyone was there, all the workers from the plantation, as well as some of the businessmen René had been close with. Though this was more of a family ceremony, René had touched a lot of people with his fairness and ability to work with everyone.

The tradition was to have a celebration with music, laughter, and food. Tears and black were unwelcome. Mary outdid herself. When Damica saw all of the wonderful food and the beautiful table, the thought crossed her mind that Mary must have cooked all day to make it all so perfect.

Somehow Damica found a plate of food in her hand. Everyone was trying to make sure she was okay, had a seat, and had some food, water, or anything she needed. Two sat on her shoulder. Favorite was nowhere to be found. She wished she could be hiding somewhere with Favorite.

She wandered into the room where René was laid out. There must have been a thousand candles all over, casting shadows throughout the room. She sat on a wooden chair and placed her plate on the floor before she bent over and wept again. They had not known each other long, but Damica knew this man was something special, someone she would miss for eternity.

The room was quiet. Only the cat and Damica were there. The shadows behind her began to move. Cat and woman turned at the same time to see a shadow of a man standing behind her, putting his hand on her shoulder. Damica could feel that it was warm, comforting. A voice floated through her head. *I told you I would always be with you.*

She jumped up, knocking the chair over as she went. The shadow stood there, across from her, still no feeling of malice, just comfort. *I'm sorry, Damica, I didn't get to tell you everything, but I'm here. In the shadows.*

"The power of darkness and dawn, I think I'm understanding part of that," Damica said softly, smiling at the shadow.

Angelica was standing just within the doorway. She seemed stunned by what she saw. Damica smiled at her and then looked back toward the shadow, but it was gone.

"Are you okay, Damica? Who are you talking to? Maybe you should go lie down. It's been a long day."

Damicas jaw hung open. Angelica had not seen him. She looked around frantically and noticed Two looking in another direction than the shadow had been in. The shadows seemed to move and come together in the form of a man, René, who she saw put a finger to his lips to tell her to be quiet. She could hear his laughter in her head, smell his scent over the jasmine. Two walked over to the shadow and tried to rub on its leg, but he just went right through it.

"Yes, I think it's time for me to go lie down. Thank you, Angelica."

She kept glancing at each shadow on the walk up to her rooms to see if he was there. Two pranced along beside her, letting her know that they were alone.

At her rooms, Damica sat on her bed. As she dropped her head into her hands, she could not believe all that had happened. She knew in her heart that she had to have hallucinated the shadow. René was no longer with her. With a heavy heart, she lifted her head to the breeze that entered through the open doors. It was then she saw him standing in front of her.

The candle was behind her, so the shadows were being cast in front of her. He reached his hand out and caressed her hair. She could feel him, she tried to place her hand over his, but it just went through him, leaving her touching her own face.

She looked up to where he was, "Can you stay with me tonight?" He nodded as she curled in bed. She kept the candle lit so the shadow would remain. She felt his arms go around her, holding her tight. She sighed in contentment and fell into a dreamless sleep.

A commotion within the house roused Damica. She hurriedly got dressed, realizing the candle had been blown out at some point in the night.

She scooped up Two and looked around for Favorite, but she was nowhere to be found.

The house was in chaos as people ran around. She headed to the kitchen to see what was going on. If anyone knew, Mary would.

"A lot of different people are coming to pay their respects, food and flowers being delivered. No one wanted to bother you, so Angelica has everyone running around getting everything in order. I think René's lawyer is coming to speak to you today, so let's get you some café au lait and a good breakfast. You may have a fight on your hands. He is more René's daddy's lawyer than René's. Be ready to stand your ground, lady.

"This is rightfully your home now! Do not let them bully you out of it. Honestly, we are all behind you. No one wants to go back to how it was when René was not in charge." The color drained out of her face, and she shook off the memory of the time before.

"I will do my best; I wish we had had time to speak of these things. Do you know if there are any papers or such I can use to help? I honestly hadn't thought of this happening. I will get on it."

"Don't worry, dear, Angelica will have it all ready for you, and she is taking care of the daily routine for now. She will help you get a handle on it as soon as there is a moment. She said you weren't feeling well last night, so she didn't want to bother you."

Damica looked down, remembering the shadow man, wondering if it was her imagination, her grief, or if she was just going crazy. She hoped against hope that it was real.

As promised, Angelica had laid all the important paperwork out on René's desk for her. Her head was bent over the paperwork when a large man burst through the door. He was as wide as he was tall. His hair was tumbled and sticking up at all angles, and he was sweating profusely. He constantly dabbed his forehead with a handkerchief. Damica guessed he was the lawyer by the frown Angelica wore standing behind him.

"Ms. Damica, I am Monsieur Lafue, Monsieur René's lawyer." Said the whale of a man, still dabbing at sweat and breathing hard as if he had run the whole way to the plantation. "I think we need to speak, in private."

He said as he looked over his shoulder at Angelica. Damica nodded at Angelica, letting her know that she would be okay.

"How may I help you, monsieur?" Damica remained seated behind the large desk. She had an inkling that her size would make this man feel the need to bully her more. And she did not feel he deserved the respect of standing.

"I am here to let you know that with the death of René, the plantation reverts back to his father and that you must vacate the premise." He wheezed the words out.

Damica was expecting this and had actually gone through all the papers that were left out. She was sure she was missing something, she was sure that René would not have left her in such a lurch, but of course, they hadn't been married very long, so it was possible.

Monsieur Lafue was rambling on as the sun shone through the large windows. Damica was not entirely paying attention, just smiling at the man, trying to figure out her next move when she saw him.

Two first let her know that the shadow man was there first. He jumped off the desk and began to purr and tried to rub on his legs. The shadow man stood beside a box on the bookshelf, trying to point at it emphatically, making a wild show of it. Damica understood immediately and smiled wider.

"Monsieur Lafue, I do believe you are mistaken. Give me just a moment to double-check something, please."

"I am not wrong. You are to leave." He began to swell his chest out as he spoke to her, standing and stomping his foot. However, she was used to people using their size to intimidate her, so it made no difference if he puffed up, stamped, or stood on a ladder for all she cared.

Damica demurely got up from the desk and slid past him to the box that René had been pointing at. She carried it over to the desk. Lafue's face went white when he saw it.

Damica opened it to see that René and his father had signed a contract. If he were to take a wife, a proper wife, the plantation would be his with no strings attached. Under this was a handwritten letter.

As she read, she realized that René had most likely known that he would die. He had made this letter very clear that his plantation would be passed on to his wife. Damica handed these to the lawyer. His face turned red, then purple.

"What... how...there is no way this will stand up in court! You cannot steal a man's land and expect to get away with it."

At this point, Damica had had enough. She was shipped halfway across the world, married a man that she actually liked, maybe even loved, who was killed by a vampire that hated her because another vampire seemed to like her. Now this *salopard* was trying to take away her new home, her new family, and the only source of income she had!

Anger and rage rolled over her as she only moved her eyes to look at him, knowing how terrifying she must have looked by the way his face paled. He took a step away toward the door as if readying for his escape.

"My husband owned the land, not his father. My husband left the land to me, not his father. My husband left all of this to me, including the people that work here, not to his father. If you want a war, Monsieur Lafue, I will give you a war."

Her voice was quiet, yet the power that came through was enough to make what color was left drain from his face.

"You know what my husband could do and what he was. I can do more." Her lip curled up as she lifted her head and stood stock still.

The anger and power pulsing around her made her look taller and more imposing. The air began to crackle, books began to fly off the shelves at him. She took a deep breath and tried to control herself. She didn't want to hurt him, just make him leave.

"I think it best if you leave, monsieur. If you have any more questions, you may address my lawyer." She strode out of the room, looking ten feet tall, out into the kitchen where Mary and Angelica stared open-mouthed at her.

"Do I really look that bad," she said as she slumped in a chair, all the air and energy draining from her, leaving her spent.

"No, you don't look bad. You have a glow about you. I mean, you are literally glowing!" Damica looked down at herself but did not see it. She thought she looked quite normal, if a bit tired. Her arms were shaking the tiniest amount, and she felt as though she would cry, then sleep, then eat everything in the kitchen. As all of this was happening, one of the housemaids came in with a letter for her. All she could do was sigh and say thank you. Mary put some food and a big glass of water in front of her.

She wasn't even sure what was on the plate, but she put the letter down and ate everything in what felt like two seconds. Mary took the plate and put another in front of her. This time she ate slowly, enjoying everything that Mary had given her. She closed her eyes and savored the cheese and bread; the water was the best thing she had put to her lips in a long time. The thought made her smile as a memory she couldn't quite catch floated through her brain.

She sighed again but this time in contentment. Then she opened her eyes and looked at the letter.

Chapter Twenty-Five

Dearest Damica,

I wish to send my condolences on the death of your husband. What a tragedy for you to have lost him so soon after you were married. I have decided that Jeanne is not stable. She went rogue when she got into a scuffle with your husband. I would love to spend some time with you when you are feeling better.

With Love,

Appolline.

Every bit of anger that had dissipated reappeared. Shaking, she crumpled the letter up and tossed it in the fire. How could that woman think she wanted to have anything to do with her! Appolline was as much a part of René's death as Jeanne was. Damica wasn't one hundred percent sure how the power structure with vampires worked, but she was sure that had Appolline wanted to, she could have stopped Jeanne at any time.

She was sure the plan had been to kill him and make Damica so helpless that she would crawl over and surrender herself to Appolline. It would be a cold day in hell before that would ever happen. She tried to take a deep breath and calm down, but she just found it made her angrier, and being angry was not a good thing right now.

Pots and pans started flying from wherever they had been put to keep safe. A knife whizzed passed her. She wasn't sure how long things had been flying around her. It was like the anger overtook her, and she lost herself in it. She looked around to see Mary and Angelica hiding under the table.

Seeing her friends so scared literally took the wind out of her sails, and everything that was in the air fell where it was.

"I'm so sorry, I'm so sorry. I'm not sure what this is. It's never happened before." Damica dropped her head into her hands and cried.

"You are coming into your powers a bit more, dear. That's all. It will take a while to adjust. Sometimes a traumatic event reveals more than you thought that you had." Mary wrapped her arms around her and comforted her.

"I was never one to have anything like you and René had, but I've seen it in a few. You will have to see what you can do and try to find what triggers this reaction. Though from the looks of it, whatever was in that letter was the trigger."

She looked around her kitchen, which was destroyed. "I think you said Grand'Mere sent a book home with you. I think you should sit and read it today. There might be something in it that can help. Go on, head over to your room, and close the door. We can keep everyone out so you can have some peace. I'll bring up something to eat in a few minutes. Go on." Damica gave her one last squeeze and headed to her room to find the book.

Mary had been right, of course. The book had a few passages at the end that were not recipes or plants. The pages here explained about power. How it came about, how it leaked, different types, but most of all, it explained or tried to explain how to harness it.

The first step is to know what type of power you possess, or what types, as many wielders have a few different flavors of power. Witches and warlocks are generally born with it but can use the power of voodoo to harness other, more remote power. Voodoo is hereditary but needs to be woken within the person. Witchcraft and voodoo can work together if exposed correctly. Both are similar, I believe, though witchcraft is from Europe and voodoo is based in Africa. Voodoo is combined with the Christian faith to help conceal it from the people that snatched the practitioners from their homes and tried to convert them to their own cult. Both can be deadly to use. You can be hung or burned for both. Both have white and black magics, though dark and light don't affect this. Some are powerful at dark, some at light. Dusk and dawn are the

merging of all these powers and can be the most beneficial for major works. It is a rare power that can work in the dark and light.

Damica thought about this and what René said, darkness and dawn. That was his power time. He said Damica was more powerful in the light since her plants grew in the light. She had to think on this since throwing dishes and books around the room with just her temper would not help her when she needed it. Maybe she was merging from just a witch to a bit more. Maybe she could be that "rare power."

Yessss; the word floated through her head. *That's what I was trying to tell you, but I ran out of time. You are more. Use the book but control your power. There is a battle still to come. You must keep them all safe, please, for me. I will teach you what I can from the shadows. I am here just look into the darkness on a bright day or in the corners that never see the full light. I am here to help. Together we can win your safety.*

Damica knew what she had to do. She had to control her emotions so the people she cared about would not get hurt. She also needed to be able to draw on that same emotion to keep them safe. She needed to store it somehow, keep it in a part of herself somewhere and close that door until it was needed.

At some point, Appolline would come calling, and it was up to her to keep not only herself safe but everyone else at the plantation. Two decided at that moment to crawl up her and hang out on her shoulder. She absentmindedly stroked him until she became aware that every time she touched him, there were tingles in her fingers. She looked to the side at him. He was smiling his little kitty smile with his eyes closed and purring as she stroked him.

She placed her hand on his head and closed her eyes. A sense of calm engulfed her. She smiled. Of course, he was her familiar. She should have known that was the truth all along. That was why he decided to stow away on a ship just to be with her. All of her fear and anger washed away. She was pretty sure that the cat could help her control her emotions enough for now until she had a good grip on how to do it herself. Her confidence soared.

The day passed with her reading and learning about what she could do, or at least what might be possible. She cross-referenced between Grand' Mere's book and the books her mother had sent with her. A lot of the information was the same.

There were a lot of different plants in her new home that had the same qualities as plants she was familiar with from France. She spent the whole night reading. Angelica brought in some food at some point, but it sat uneaten on her dresser.

Whenever she wasn't sure of something, she looked toward the shadows. René was right there to help her move in the right direction. He reminded her of their lesson the other day. He made sure she understood the importance of the cardinal directions and how the song kept cadence for the magic. It wasn't long before she knew how to intertwine the two flavors of magic to make one powerful essence.

Two sat with her and purred the whole time. There was still no sign of Favorite, which made Damica sad. She wished she could have René's cat when the shadows were at bay.

She must have fallen asleep on her reading table at some point because when she woke, the sun was shining through the windows, and her face was down on the notes she had taken. She lifted her head and rubbed the side of her face that had been on the papers. Her hand came away with ink on it. *Great*, she thought, hoping she did not smear the ink, then hoping her face wasn't covered in it as well.

She got up and opened the French doors to the balcony, stretching out the kinks in her back and neck as she went. She stepped out and noticed a bouquet of flowers sitting on the railing; roses, daisies, and some bougainvillea all mixed in.

She stepped closer, but as she did, Two flew out the door hissing and growling. He stopped at the flowers and batted something out of them, then proceeded to bat the whole bouquet off the balcony. He placed his paw on top of the paper he had knocked out and looked up at her.

"Thank you, Two." She smiled and picked the cat up, and snuggled him. He purred and perched himself on her shoulder as she bent to pick the paper up.

My Dearest Damica,

I heard through the grapevine that you had a small issue with the solicitor yesterday. I can take care of that for you, just say the word. I cannot wait to see your beautiful face. Please don't wait to get back to me. There is so much that I want to share with you.

With Love Always,

Appolline

Damica just sighed and folded the note up. She walked back inside and tossed it on her writing table just as there was a knock at the door. Angelica opened the door and stuck her face in.

"Hey, I brought up a cafe au lait and some toast with honey. You didn't eat much yesterday. I thought you could use it."

Damica smiled at her friend, "Come in. I hope you made enough to stay and chat a bit. I think we need to talk about how to run this place. I'm afraid I'm being lax and letting things slide."

"Of course, I brought extra," she chuckled, "I hope all your research helped a bit and that you're feeling better. We are doing fine, getting the crops and animals taken care of. We may need to secure the shield a bit more, and we will need someone to go into the city and negotiate sales of the product. I can go with you and help, but no one will deal with me."

The rest of the morning was spent learning how the plantation ran. Damica and Angelica made plans needed to sell the crops and a list of the workers that could help keep things organized. Damica understood that she had to be the face of the business but that she really did not understand how it ran.

She proposed to Angelica that they split the profits as evenly as possible with all the workers and staff. She wanted everyone to profit from their hard work. Even though that was not how things usually worked, Damica thought she seemed to go against the norm her whole life, so why not do it in a way that would help out the people she cared most about.

"Let's make sure you get to keep it first. I think you need your own solicitor. Maybe you should head into the city this afternoon and see if you can find someone."

Two chirped at this idea, and the plans were made. Damica was excited to be heading back to the city, even if it was for business.

Chapter Twenty-Six

A storm was rolling off in the distance as Damica walked down the bustling, dusty road of Rue Royal in New Orleans. One of the housemen, Gerard, had come with her to drive as well as to make sure she was safe and knew where she was going. Gerard was a younger man, closer to Damicas age. He was an excellent driver and knew his way around the city.

"How are you so familiar with the city, Gerard?"

"René used to take me with him all the time. He let me listen in to the meetings and taught me how to figure out the profits on the crops. He made sure we could all read, but I really am interested in the numbers."

He smiled so big Damica knew that he would be her right-hand man on running the business side of things. A man slammed into Damica, knocking her to the ground.

"Watch where you are going!" he hollered at her as he strode away. Gerard helped her up and tried to dust her off as another man came out of the building and offered her a hand.

"I saw the whole thing; I am so sorry, Madame. Please come in and rest a moment. Your man can wait out here."

"No, thank you, I'm fine."

"Madame. ...., please come in and sit a moment. I knew René, it would be an honor if you would rest a moment."

At that moment, it seemed as though the shadows from the buildings began to move. Damica and Gerard exchanged a look, and he nodded slightly, used to being treated this way.

He had not seen the shadows; he was just letting her know this man was safe and she should go. She nodded and followed the man inside.

"I was hoping you would stop by. René had some papers for you," said the man, bustling about with nervous energy. He retrieved a chair for Damica and set it next to his desk, then proceeded to pour her a glass of water.

"I'm sorry, I don't quite understand. Who are you?" She was grateful for the water yet a little hesitant.

"Oh, oh right." He chuckled uncomfortably, "My name is Myles, Myles LaFontáne. I was René's solicitor." He leaned back on his heels and grinned at her. Damica just sat for a moment staring open-mouthed at him.

"Sir, I'm not sure what you are doing, but I met René's solicitor yesterday. He was not a pleasant man."

"Yes, madame, you met the man who claims to be René's solicitor, only that was actually René's father's solicitor." He smiled as big as the day with a smug look on his face. "I am the one that drew up your marriage papers the day you left the nun's home with René I also drew up the documents stating that all the property was to be handed over to you in the event of René's death.

"He was quite adamant about that. Came in last week sometime. Did you find them, or do you need a copy?"

He started sorting through the papers on his desk, looking for another copy of the documents the shadow had pointed out to her. Damica was dumbfounded. As well as ecstatic. There were so many emotions flying through her that she burst into tears.

"Oh dear, oh dear, please don't cry, Madame." He handed her a handkerchief that had obviously seen better days and used a piece of paper to fan her.

"Sir, you have no idea how happy I am to find you, to just stumble upon you. Yes, they are trying to take the plantation from me, and yes, I need your help.

"I also am looking for someone to help with the business part of the plantation. Would you be able to do that as well?"

He nodded with a smile, sighed in relief that she had stopped crying, and went on to explain that he was already set up to help keep things on the up and up.

Damica explained about sharing the profits with the workers, and the solicitor was thrilled with that idea. By the time she left his office, she had a copy of her marriage certificate that showed it was legal, a promise to get the papers about the profit sharing together, and another promise to help her fight René's father in court if needed. Damica could have floated all the way home.

She stepped out into the light of the setting sun to find Gerard. She ran to him and hugged him, which startled the young man, and he laughed. She realized how inappropriate that must be, so she looked around, hoping no one was watching. She saw two shadows stretching out from the side of the building where Gerard stood. The second shadow gave a little nod and a small wave with his hand, then disappeared.

Damica knew René had somehow made sure this was where she would stop for help.

The carriage ride back to the house was shorter than one would think but long enough, especially as the night got deeper around them. The road was dirt and full of ruts. There were swamps on each side of the road full of sounds. The croaks of frogs, the deep guttural sounds of the alligators calling to each other, and the buzz of mosquitos were the constant background to the night's serenade. Damica was enjoying the swamp-music when it suddenly stopped. Not even a mosquito was buzzing.

"Gerard, is there any way to hurry a bit more?"

"Madame, we are going as fast as we can. I hear it too. The horses are getting a bit nervous, and I don't want to run them outright. There's a chance they will panic and take off. Is there anything you can do? I know we are a moving target, but I don't think it's smart to hold still right now."

Damica could feel the air pressure change. She took a deep breath and blew it out, closing her eyes and focusing her thoughts. One more deep breath, and she set her intention. With all she could, she tried to make the carriage, its inhabitants, and the horses invisible.

She could just distinguish a swirl of dirt ahead in the road, like a small dust devil. With her otherness, she could tell there was a person standing in the middle of it.

"Stop the carriage, hold still, don't talk or move and try to keep the horses steady," Damica whispered.

She knew holding still in the dark on a road in the swamp was not really the best decision, but she wasn't sure she could hide them if they were moving. In her mind, she drew a circle around the carriage and imagined a bubble going up that no one could see through. She drew in all her breath and imagined that sound would go inside of her with that breath so no one could hear them. She pushed out the intention for whoever was there to walk past them, not acknowledge the change in the air that signified there was anything on the road with them.

She did something she had only read about. She called on the four cardinal directions and asked for assistance. She pushed out her intention further than it had ever been pushed before. She tried to intertwine her magic with what she had learned of René's.

There were no shadows or cat to help, only herself and her intentions. She held on to her amulet and opened her eyes. It was fully dark by now, so there was always a chance that whatever it was on the road would not notice them anyways. At least, Damica thought that until she heard the voice.

"Come out, little witch. I know you are here somewhere; I can smell you. Your fear, your sweat, your blood." Drawled out Jeanne as she walked closer and closer to the carriage.

Damica wasn't sure if she could actually smell them. She wasn't sure how to stop that. Her heart was racing as Jeanne came closer to them.

She did the best she could to put all her power into the shield to send the vampire away, or at least to make her not *need* to come closer.

Damica thought about everything this thing had done to her since she first saw her, and the intention got stronger. She felt the click of power as the Lao answered her prayers to them. She did her best to make both flavors of power work together to keep them safe.

"I can hear your little heart pitter-patter. Is that how she makes you feel. Do you think you can steal her from me and not pay any consequences!" This last part came out almost as a roar. Damica flinched but held up her shield.

Jeanne continued to walk down the lane until she was even with the carriage. They both held their breath as she passed by, hoping that no fly would bother the horses and make them shake or stomp. The darkness worked in their favor as no shadows were cast.

Jeanne soon got angry at not being able to find them. She stomped her foot and raised her fist in their direction. For just a second, Damicas heart stopped, and she thought they had been found.

"You may think you can hide from me, little witch, but I will find you!" And with that, she seemed to take off like a shot into the sky and was gone.

Damica collapsed in the carriage, and the world around them seemed to start up again. The night sounds seemed deafening as the horses started to snort and stomp. It didn't take much encouragement to get Gerard to move the horses on. They trotted as fast as they could on the dark road trying to get to the house's safety.

Home looked peaceful as they were racing toward the house. Lights were shining in the windows of the cabins and the big house. Gerard stopped at the house to let her out, then hurried on to the stable to take care of the horses. Damica made him promise to head straight to his home after that and to try to keep everyone inside for the night if possible.

The cattle were still being kept close to the cabins for safety, and no one ventured outside after dark anymore, even if some of the animals hadn't made it to the safety of the corral at dusk. Everyone was very aware of what could happen.

Two sat on the porch like an old impatient mother waiting for her late ward. He yowled at her and looked out at the night as if to say, *How could you even chance it.*

"I know, I know, it was stupid of me to be out so late. But Two! René was so smart and wonderful! He set it all up. We are here to stay, and it is ours, ours to do with as we please and ours to share with whom we wish!"

She scooped the cat up and spun around on the porch with him. He snuggled into her neck, purring so loud it drowned out the rest of the night's sounds. Mary popped her head out the door just as she was spinning back toward it.

"My goodness, child, you had us all worried! Get in here and get something to eat. You look pale. Did something happen? Oh lord, my mind goes to the worst possible thing, but seeing you out here dancing with that cat makes me think it could not be the worst."

"Well, we had a run-in with one of the vampires, but, oh my goodness, did I find out some great news for all of us! Let's go in and chat while I grab something to eat."

They headed in, Two purring in her arms. The three ladies shared a meal in the kitchen while Damica told them all the good news from the lawyer. There were tears and cheers, hugs and whoops. It took all that was in them not to run out to the cabins and share the news, but they knew tonight would be spent in the big house. No one was walking through the dark this night.

Chapter Twenty-Seven

After the small celebration, the ladies headed to their rooms. Damica took a moment to say a quiet thank you to René, hoping to see his shadow as she spoke, but he was nowhere about. She reluctantly turned toward her bed, where Two was getting settled for the night, right in the middle of the pillows, and again, no sign of Favorite. The evening was when the little cat was missed the most. Damica hoped that with René's death, nothing had happened to her. She was hoping to take care of her the way he would have.

She settled down and blew out the candle. She was confident that nothing could bother her tonight. Her house was protected, as were her people, and soon she drifted off to sleep, spent from the day.

The moonlight was streaming through the closed doors from the balcony. Damica could not figure out what had awakened her until she heard the stones hit the door again. She sat up groggily in bed. Two was already at the door. His hair was all puffed up, so she knew to be cautious, if nothing else.

"Damica." The whisper seemed to float around the room, "My love, come out and see me. I have been waiting for you."

Damica froze midway out of bed, she did not want to go out and confront Appolline, nor did she think it was a good idea to continue to ignore her. At some point, things were going to get deadlier than they already had been.

She closed her eyes and imagined René's smile, his laugh, the gentleness with which he handled the children on the plantation. Her anger began to grow and boil under her skin. She thought about Marie and all the crewmen that had died on the ship, about the animals that had gone missing, including Favorite kitty.

She felt a shift within herself and got up slowly. She put on a pair of René's pants instead of her own skirt. She bent down at her knees and felt how easy the movement was. She found a loose top, put it on with the pants, and tossed away her nightgown. Now for shoes. René had left a pair of boots by the back door that no one had the heart to move. She had noticed them earlier in the day before she had left for town. She scooped Two up and placed him on her shoulders. She swooped her hair up in a band to keep it out of her face and headed down the stairs to find the boots.

The boots were too big, as were the pants. She tucked some kitchen towels inside the front of the boots, then tucked the pants inside the top. She didn't hurry. She was sure Appolline would be waiting no matter how much time she took to get outside.

She looked around the kitchen, wondering if there was any use taking a knife with her. She really didn't want to get that close to the vampire, and she didn't know how to stab a person. She opted on using her own strength and power. She sent a little prayer to the powers that be that the moon was strong enough to produce shadows and stepped outside the house.

Two was hyper-aware of everything in the night, which was rather annoying with him still on her shoulder. His little paws were digging into her. She thought about tossing him off of her but then thought better of it. Not only was he helpful with her power, but the little bit of pain might just keep her grounded as long as it wasn't all she concentrated on.

The night was unusually bright, the moon was full, and the sky was clear. The humidity was lower today, so the air felt almost cool to her skin. She walked confidently around to the front of the house. She couldn't help but appreciate the freedom of movement the pants lent her, but the shirt she found to be a bit loose and slightly in the way. She made note to see if she could have a set like this made in her size. If she made it through the night, that is.

She heard a whisper of her name as it floated on the breeze. It seemed to be pulling her somewhere. She was aware of the pull and allowed herself to go that way. She could have stopped it had she chosen to. The force led her out into the marshy area around the front of the property, away from everyone and everything else.

The frogs and crickets were in full racket, and the smell of earthy decay was all around as she stepped under the live oak trees. The Spanish moss swung from the trees creating elaborate shadows on the ground. She could see a small opening in the trees ahead of her. Damica followed the call to it. Standing in the middle of the opening was Appolline.

"This is a bit dramatic, don't you think." Damica wasn't sure if it was the smartest thing she had ever said in her life, but to be honest, she was so tired of this.

Tired of the fear, the grief, and just the game-playing. She wasn't sure if this would be the end for her, just that she was done taking any more crap.

"Damica, my love, you've come to me." She opened her arms in a welcoming way. Damica felt the pull grow stronger. She shrugged it off. The look on Appolline's face was priceless. No one had ever been able to resist her call so thoroughly before.

"My love, whatever is the matter? I thought you would want to be with me, spend eternity together."

"Please don't try that, Appolline. I felt the pull. You weren't counting on me wanting you. You were counting on me being weak, or at least weak enough to have to follow you."

Appolline's face turned to shock as she tried her best to look hurt by the words, but Damica could feel the rage boiling right under the surface.

Two let out a small sound as if to remind her to watch herself. She reached up and gave the cat a scratch to let him know she understood, then took a breath and stood resolute before the vampire.

"Well," Appolline sighed as if offended, "there's no reason to be rude. I just thought you might want to see me as much as I wanted to see you."

She started to circle around Damica casually, as though she wasn't planning anything, just needed to pace.

"Your girl tried to kill me today."

"And who would my girl be?"

"Jeanne. She's hunting me, I believe. She's dangerous. You should really do something about her.'

"Psht, she is not mine. And yes, she probably is a little dangerous. You should really find a place that will keep you safe."

Damica could feel the pull start, only this time, she had had enough. With the snap of her fingers, the pull was broken like a string drawn too tight. Appolline was rocked back by the feel of pull jumping back at her. Her face contorted in rage.

"How dare you! I kept you alive! How dare you not repay me!" The words boomed, shaking the trees and producing a wind that hadn't been there before.

Damica looked up to watch the trees and draw on the energy that was being produced. There, up in the highest branches, she saw a figure. Jeanne, she was sure of it. What she wasn't sure of was what side she would fall on if a fight happened.

"I kept myself alive along with the other girls. You cooperated. That's it. I could have kept us safe with or without you."

A snarl came from Appolline, her face contorted in such a way that the monster within was visible.

"You are mine!" she shouted.

The shadow man appeared and pushed Damica down as Jeanne careened off the trees, growling and snarling like a wild beast. Damica hit the ground somewhat harder than she expected. Two had launched himself off of Damica and landed on his feet in front of her just as the two vampires collided. Damica sat up, blood pouring from a wound on her arm, the shadow put its hand over the wound, and the bleeding stopped.

The battle of the two vampires raged on across the clearing. They resembled two wild animals clawing and biting. The ground grew black with all the blood being spilled and sprayed.

Damica considered turning and walking away, but she thought better of it. Best to deal with it tonight when the moon was full, and the shadows could help.

She began to chant to the cardinal directions, calling on the Lao again for help. She pulled on her own inner strength to match the power she hoped to gain from the Lao. She had already asked for too much today without giving a gift. She looked around for something worthy of them, then took some of the blood-soaked earth in her hand, lifted it over her head, offering it to them. The dirt began to swirl and move, then was lifted out of her hands. Immediately she felt a shock go through her body as the power surged within her.

Jeanne was like a wild animal, attacking Appolline, who was holding her own until Jeanne slapped her so hard she flew across the ground, twisting and turning as she went. Small trees and bushes were torn up as she scraped over them.

"You, you tried to replace me with her! Why," Jeanne started sobbing, "I have been loyal to you for centuries. I have loved you through everything. I have stood by while you got us kicked out of France, while you brought in lovers here and there over the years. Why would you choose her! Look at her. She is nothing. Small and mortal."

She broke down and dropped to her knees. Damica couldn't help but feel bad for her. She knew what it was like to have her heart broken though she would have killed to spend centuries with René.

"I'm sorry, Jeanne, I didn't want any of this," Damica whispered, hoping she could hear her sincerity.

Jeanne, her hands still covering her face, stopped sobbing and just seemed to take a breath. She looked up at Damica. Her eyes were red from crying, blood tears streaked her face. "I know, I know. I can see that now. You were just trying to live your life, as was I when she found me. You are stronger than I was. We have no quarrel here."

Damica thought about this, about how Jeanne killed Marie and René. How she made everyone she cared about terrified. She might have no quarrel now, but that did not mean there was no quarrel at all. Still, Damica nodded. It had all stemmed from Appolline. She was who the fight was with tonight.

Jeanne stood up and swung at Appolline, who saw it coming and threw a punch so hard it sent Jeanne flying through the air. A tree stopped her mid-flight, and she slid to the ground. Her breath came out in gurgles as blood poured out of her mouth. A branch protruded from her chest, right where her heart should have been.

Her eyes were wide when they looked at Damica, then in an instant, they clouded over whatever life force she had possessed seemed to vanish. Appolline slowly approached the body. She reached out as if afraid to touch her, then let out a whimper and covered her mouth with her hands.

"Jeanne, Jeanne. No, Jeanne! No!"

She whirled around on Damica so fast that there was no way to see the full movement.

"You! You ruined everything!" Appolline screamed as she launched herself at Damica.

Damica had just enough time to throw herself out of the way, leaving Appolline to fly into the woods behind her. Damica turned and threw out her hands. Two had climbed back up to perch on her shoulder, hissing and growling in the direction the vampire had gone.

She threw her power to where she could feel the vampire approaching. Purple light shot from her hands and hit the vampire square in the chest, knocking her back into the trees. Damica stumbled back. She had used too much power. She needed to pace herself, even with the cat and the Lao there to help.

She stared into the darkness waiting for the vampire to appear. There was nothing. Maybe she ran away or was hurt beyond repair. Maybe she was dead. Then a weight landed on top of Damica, and her world went haywire.

The shield cracked, sending the cat flying. Appolline sat on her back, crushing her face into the earth. It was getting hard to breathe. Between the weight on her ribs and the dirt she was breathing in, black spots began to appear around her vision.

Appolline seemed to be thrown off her, and she rolled onto her back as she gulped in air. She wasn't sure if it was from a lack of oxygen or if she was really seeing this. The shadow was solid, fighting the vampire in hand-to-hand combat.

I can't hold this too long. Can you get up? the words floated through her mind. She nodded and slowly got to her feet, mentally doing a health check. Ribs, sore. Throat, raw. Pride, wounded.

She tried again for a shield sending it up only for it to flicker. She sighed, closed her eyes, and concentrated on protecting herself. The shield snapped into place. She opened her eyes in time to see the vampire throw a ball of what looked like fire at the shadow man, and he vaporized.

"NO!" the scream ripped from her throat as she watched the particle of shadow float off into the night.

All the memories slammed into her, filling her with rage and fire. Standing as tall as she could, her lip lifted into a sneer, eyes slanted in concentration and pure rage, appearing deadlier than any vampire, she marched off toward the vampire, hurling power at her as she went.

Appolline was shocked and retreated to the edge of the woods, but that didn't last long. Soon the vampire was shrugging off the power, though it was taking a toll on her.

The two women converged on each other, Damica launching herself at Appolline. Two launched right alongside her. His power surrounded him. It gave Damica the boost she needed. The vampire grabbed hold of the cat and flung him away. Damica could hear his bones snap as he hit the tree. The power they had shared was severed.

She didn't have time to look or to mourn another loss. Her power was now lessened with the shadow and the cat gone. But the rage. The rage that boiled inside her had just been fed a gourmet meal with the loss of her beloved cat. Damica hit the vampire with the force of a thousand pounds. She picked her up and threw the vampire just as she had thrown Two.

Tears welled up in Damicas eyes at the idea of her lost cat. She launched herself again at the vampire, this time calling on the four cardinal directions for guidance, as she had learned from René. Her own natural powers, which she had cultivated with the help of Grand'Mere's writings, merged with the Voodoo she had learned. The power flashed to a deep dark red as it emanated from her body, decimating everything in its wake.

The trees bowed to her whim, the wind itself seemed to explode from her, tearing out the grass, tossing rocks and tree stumps. Appolline threw her arms up, trying to protect herself, but the onslaught of power dropped her to her hands and knees. Damica approached her, encircling her in the eye of the hurricane that was her power.

Damica reached down and grabbed the vampire by her hair, dragging her partially to her feet. Appolline clawed at her, raking her flesh and ripping open another wound on her arm. Damica wrapped her free hand around the vampire's neck.

"Go ahead and squeeze my love. You can't kill me. I am immortal!" She wheezed out a laugh.

Damica squeezed, calling again on the cardinal directions, but this time she added her own spin.

"North, South, East, and West. I implore you to guide my hand. I implore the powers and being of the night and darkness to coerce this life force to be no more!"

With that, she took a deep breath in, jammed her knee as far as she could into the vampire's diaphragm, and blew out the power of the darkness into the vampire. She watched as the shock and realization flashed across Appolline's face. She opened her mouth to scream, but only a black mass released from her that floated above their heads.

The life began to fade from the vampire's eyes. Under Damicas hands, the body began to turn to dust. Damica stepped back, letting the body fall out of the eye and back into the storm itself.

The mass held steady over her, moving as she moved. She had taken the immortal life force from a vampire using a mixture of different types of dark magic. She now had to pay the price. She lifted her head and raised her arms and eyes to the mass.

It engulfed her, swirling with the storm she had created until it descended upon her. Her body fell heavily to the damp ground, the storm abruptly stopped. The moon hid behind a cloud, and darkness descended.

Chapter Twenty-Eight

She could hear hushed voices coming from somewhere close, the purr of a cat accompanied by the patting of its paw on her hand made her open her eyes.

"Two?" she croaked out the words, realizing she was parched. As she focused, she realized that it was not Two. It was Favorite. She had come back after all. Damica stroked Favorite's soft fur, speaking quietly to let her know she had been missed. Afraid to tell the cat that her companion was no more. She heard the creak as her door opened, and Angelica peeked in.

"Hi, it's good to see you awake." She walked slowly toward the bed. "Can I get you anything?" Damica could tell she had been crying as she laid her hand gently on Damicas other hand. The cat still claimed the one.

"Water, please."

"Of course, let me help you sit up."

With some grunting and struggling and perhaps a giggle or two, they got Damica into sitting position so she could be given a large glass of water.

"Not too fast. The doctor said you should just take a few sips to make sure you don't get sick." Damica nodded and tried not to gulp the whole glass down.

"Do you know what happened?" Damica nodded but didn't say anything. "We found you in the woods, in René's clothes. You were lying there, staring up at the sky. You didn't move or respond. We thought you were dead until you took a breath and screamed.

"You wouldn't stop screaming until I gathered you in my arms and rocked you back and forth. The ground was bloody. There was a big pile of ash about ten feet from you. I had to get some help to carry you back. You have been asleep for three days now. We were afraid you wouldn't make it, and..." She trailed off, a tear rolling down her cheek.

"I'm here. Alive. In a way, at least." She smiled at her friend and noticed that the sun was full and the sky was clear through the French doors.

She looked down at herself, wondering exactly what had happened. She had felt the blackness enter her body. It engulfed her soul. She felt the battle inside rage on as her existence fought with it.

She remembered seeing the night sky turn into day, felt the dew on her skin, but she could not move.

The battle continued to rage on inside her until she seemed to float away. The world had gone black until the little cat had urged her to wake. She wasn't sure which had won; it seemed the sun did not bother her, and she was thirsty. At no point had Appolline ever eaten or had anything to drink when they had dined together on the boat.

Her thoughts were interrupted by Angelica's next words.

"Then we found Two. He was so broken. He is a fighter, though. He has made it through the last few days. I'm not sure how much longer he can hold on. He seems to have lost a lot of blood, and when I say broken, it's as if every bone in his little body was snapped. He is taking in water and broth, but that's all we can get him to take." A tear slid down her cheek as she told Damica about her beloved cat.

"Please, may I see him?"

Angelica helped her out of bed, she had no strength to walk, but she had to see that little cat one more time. They managed to get to the kitchen, where he was lying by the hearth.

Tears streamed down her face as she placed her hand on his broken body. He opened his eyes and let out a small meow, then closed his eyes.

Damica knew he had waited to see if she was okay. At that last moment, she scooped him up and ran with him outside, stumbling as she went. She held him ever so gently so his shadow would be cast on the ground. Then with all her will, she said the last words René had said, "Darkness and dawn, as the shadows lay across the ground, so shall you."

He took one last breath, and then her little Two was gone. She collapsed on the ground and sobbed. She had not cried for René yet or the loss of her mother, or any of it.

The loss of her friend, her familiar, broke her, and she sobbed until there was nothing left. When she was through, with just a few tears making their way down her cheeks, she took his body and buried him under the Bougainvillea bush that wound its way up toward her room.

She refused food, she did take a glass of water though and headed up to her room. There was nothing left for her today. She was done. She slogged up the stairs and opened her door. There on her bed sat Favorite. She was so happy to see the little white and grey cat she almost missed the tiny kitten. Damica genuinely smiled, for there sleeping right where her shoulder would have been was a tiny brown tabby with white on his nose. He looked up at her with sleepy eyes and let out a small meow. He looked just like his dad.

Epilogue.

The sun shone brightly as Damica drank her Cafe Au Lait. She loved sitting at Cafe DuMonde and watching the tourists wander around taking photos. A lot had changed from the time she first arrived in New Orleans, most good, but not all of it.

She missed all the marsh and farmland, but she appreciated the freedoms that her family were now allowed. Her mind wandered to the night it had all changed. No one had ever found evidence of Jeanne's remains by the tree. No body or pile of ash. Somehow the vampire had gotten up and walked away from the scene. It could have happened at any time, while they had been battling each other or while Damica had been battling the darkness inside her.

In a sense, she had beat the darkness, she was still herself, but since that time, she had not aged or died. Hundreds of years had gone by, and here she was, watching the tourists eating beignets and drinking coffee.

She hated to call it Au Lait since it was nothing like that wonderful concoction that Mary used to make for her.

The closest she could figure was that the black mass had been the vampire's life force, it had tried to take over Damica, but her bloodline was too powerful, so it just left her immortal with none of the side effects.

She could walk in the sun, and there was no drinking of blood. Those were all good things; the bad things were watching everyone she cared for age and die. She had seen the end to slavery, and given the plantation completely over to the family, they had run it successfully, and all the descendants were very well to do now.

She smiled as she thought how happy René would be to see this. She still kept track of them, she liked to see how they were doing, and when they hit a rough spot, she would find a way to help them out.

Damica had traveled back to France once it had gotten easier to do. She had seen where her mother was buried and said a silent thank you to the woman that had set this all in motion. To be honest, she was quite happy with her life. She spent a good part of it hunting down rogue vampires, always on the lookout for Jeanne. She had come close to catching her a time or two, but they had never crossed paths again. Damica was pretty sure this was Jeanne's plan.

After she had killed Appolline, other extraordinaire had come to her seeking help and advice. No one had ever taken down a vampire as powerful as that before.

There was no one else in the world with the powers that Damica had, vampire immortality, voodoo, and witch magic. She thought it was her duty to help out anyone who needed it when dealing with the more deadly of the extraordinaire.

Her familiar was still from Two's line, her current cat, Jaho, was the spitting image of Two. Okay, maybe she was a bit fatter than Two had been. Damica wasn't too fond of Jaho sitting on her shoulder. It tended to leave bruises.

As the line had gone on, the power within the cats increased. Now if Jaho sneezed the wrong way, a puff of blue could be seen issuing from her, increasing whatever was going on around her. Plants grew bigger, people fought harder or loved harder. She had a great influence on those around her.

Since that night, Damica rarely wore dresses or gowns. She loved the era she was in now, Ox blood Doc Martins, skinny black jeans, a retro Joan Jett T-shirt all under a black leather jacket. She loved seeing how far fashion had come, though she missed the 1920' men's fashions. Too many men now wore super tight pants or sagged them so you could see their undies. Damica crinkled her nose at the thought of this.

Her iPhone rang in her pocket, another amazing item from this era. She slid her finger across the screen and answered it.

"Yeah, go."

The caller was part of the coalition of witches that hunted down rogue vampires. She was off on another hunting mission. She chugged the last of her coffee and dropped a few dollars on the table. Jaho jumped into her arms.

The sun was shining brightly as they walked away. Anyone paying a bit of attention would have noticed not only the shadow of the girl holding the cat but the shadows of the man and the cat that seemed to dance along behind them in the sun.

Don't miss out!

Visit the website below and you can sign up to receive emails whenever Terry Hooker publishes a new book. There's no charge and no obligation.

https://books2read.com/r/B-A-NSGX-FIDMC

BOOKS 2 READ

Connecting independent readers to independent writers.

About the Author

About the Author: Terry Hooker is a bestselling author, freelance writer and editor, a Jersey girl from the shore turned Florida farm girl. She has a BA in anthropology, an AAS in Culinary Arts, and an MA in Library science. She has worked as a congressional archivist, historian, teacher, and professional chef and has presented her research on the history and iconography of southern cemeteries throughout the Southeast United States. She has edited several children's books, full length novels, dissertations, and academic papers; Terry, herself, has published scholarly papers, magazine articles, fictional stories, and books. She lives with her husband, two kids, and a plethora of critters.

You can follow her on Instagram: https://www.instagram.com/thooker_author or facebook: https://www.facebook.com/Terry-Hooker-Author

Milton Keynes UK
Ingram Content Group UK Ltd.
UKHW010854040923
428018UK00004B/448